Uncle Whiskers

Philip Brown has been a naturalist and countryman all his life. During the seventeen years for which he was Secretary of the Royal Society for the Protection of Birds, and subsequently editor of *Shooting Times and Country Magazine*, he has been concerned with bringing sportsmen and conservationists together in a no-nonsense approach to a common cause. His previous books include *Birds of Prey* and *Birds in the Balance*.

Uncle Whiskers

PHILIP BROWN

FONTANA/COLLINS

First published by André Deutsch Limited 1974
First issued in Fontana 1977

Copyright © Philip Brown 1974

Made and printed in Great Britain by
William Collins Sons & Co Ltd Glasgow

This book is dedicated, in respect and high regard, to the Veterinary Surgeons of this country. A more skilful and devoted body of men and women it would be hard to find and had they not existed Uncle Whiskers would never have lived his full, long and exciting life and this book could never have been written.

Author's Note

Uncle Whiskers was born in July 1959 and died in his fourteenth year, on 4 October 1972. At the time of his death I was hundreds of miles away but that evening a friend who had looked after him for the last six years of his life called me up on the telephone and said: 'This has been a very sad day.'

'Uncle Whiskers is dead?' 'Yes,' she replied and I realized she was very close to tears. 'Don't cry,' I answered. 'He has had a wonderful life and nobody could have done more for him than you have.'

It seemed absurd to weep over the passing of a cat. I didn't, although Uncle Whiskers had been a unique cat. I bought half a dozen daffodil bulbs and, some three weeks later, I visited his grave, marked by a circle of limestones, under an ash tree where he used to doze away the hours of many a warm summer's afternoon. Within the small circle of grey stones I planted my daffodil bulbs, pressing them firmly down with a foot. This was my last tribute to a courageous, enterprising and intelligent animal for which I had developed, over the years, both admiration and affection. I knew that Uncle Whiskers had never bothered about daffodils but they blow in spring, when the warmer days return and there is all the promise of the summer ahead. Uncle Whiskers loved the sunshine and warmth of summer, especially so in his old age.

As I turned away after completing my simple task I muttered, *sotto voce*, 'Good-bye, Uncle Whiskers.' In that moment I thought I heard an answering call – the lisping mew with which Uncle Whiskers had always greeted one and all. I even turned round but there was nothing except the stones above the grave, the stone steps down to the little wicket-gate through which he had sometimes made his escape to the big, wide world beyond and the autumn breeze sighing in the dry, fading leaves of the ash tree which had shaded him from the hot sun of many a summer's day.

The world was momentarily blurred for me as I walked away up the path. Is it really so absurd to be moved by the death of a cat? I must leave readers to pass judgement after they have read this biography of Uncle Whiskers, a cat whose courage, intelligence, patience and enterprise enabled him to get much more fun out of life with two legs than the majority of cats ever do with their full complement of four.

Before the Advent

I have known a few cats in my time but I should be dishonest if I gave the impression that I am bowled over by them. Every cat, like every dog, has some sort of a personality of its own (although it isn't *necessarily* a pleasant personality) but, as with men and women, you need more than a casual acquaintance with any cat or dog before you can even begin to understand how they 'tick'.

Cats tend to be rather aloof with strangers; dogs tend to be rather friendly (although one should never bank on this maxim if one is trying to ingratiate oneself with, say, a strange Border terrier). My wife, the daughter of a farmer, was a great girl for cats. They always had three or four cats to cull the rats and mice. I wasn't really interested in any of them but if you are courting the hand of a fair lady you are well advised to mind your p's and q's. I did my best, anyway, to convey the impression that I thought cats were rather good fun. In fact I did begin to appreciate that, apart from their grace of movement and often beautifully marked fur coats, most cats had characters of their own, even if some of their personalities were disagreeably unpleasant.

One such character was Judy. She was a thick-set, muscular tortoiseshell who played havoc with rats, mice, rabbits and birds. She was the nearest approach to a wild cat that ever condescended to live – at least part-time – indoors. She ate indoors and slept indoors but the weather had to be vile to tempt her to stay in at night. Nobody dared touch her and if anybody tried to get her out of her kitchen chair she would unroll in a flash, spitting and snarling, and slash at the intruder's hand with needle-sharp claws fully extended.

When I got married my wife introduced two cats to the household. One of these was a small, very pretty and very quiet tortoiseshell. She was much admired by the males and had already produced several litters of kittens, not one of which had been considered to be worth its keep. But just before I joined the RAF after the outbreak of Hitler's war she presented us with a ginger kitten which we decided to keep. I rather missed out on the formative years of this fine cat, to which we had given the name of Timothy. When I enlisted we packed up our few sticks of furniture and my wife went to stay with her parents for the duration. On one of my leaves I put up an enormous 'black'.

Timothy often used to go out hunting after dark, winter or summer. By using a devious route over outhouses and the kitchen roof he could land on the narrow sill of my wife's bedroom window at the back of the house. On this occasion I had arrived home on leave after a long and tedious journey, dead-tired. It was midwinter and very cold, with an inch or two of snow covering the ground. I woke from a deep sleep in the small hours and became aware of tappings on the window and, against the clear, starry sky, the vague form of the cat. I got cautiously out of bed, so as not to wake my better half and, still half-asleep, opened the window, swinging it outwards to let the happy wanderer in. Unfortunately I failed to realize that he was on the narrow ledge immediately outside that part of the window I was opening. I pushed him off and he disappeared into space. Momentarily horrified, I let out an exclamation that woke my wife. When I explained what had happened she rushed downstairs and I followed, somewhat red-faced. As soon as the back-door was opened Timothy ambled into the kitchen, shook the snow off and lapped up a saucerful of milk, none the worse for his misadventure. I simply did not realize in those days that a cat can fall fifteen or twenty feet (and probably more) without coming to any harm.

When the war was over my wife and I were lucky enough to get the lease of a dream cottage tucked away in a wooded solitude on the borders of Berkshire and Hampshire. The ginger, Timothy, was now six years old and I had not had much chance to get to know him. However, he was an affable creature and we rubbed along well enough together. It was a remote home and there was little or no traffic on the gravel lane and Timothy had a high old time hunting mice and shrews. He also developed a hatred (which was heartily reciprocated) for a tabby by the name of Sammy who lived at a cottage about half a mile away and was, in fact, his nearest feline neighbour. Both cats were big and strong and they had some rare old scraps. They were pretty evenly matched, so that whichever one happened to be doing battle on his own territory would usually see the other one off. Curiously enough both Timothy and Sammy, except when they were fighting one another, were gentle enough.

After six or seven years we moved to a village near Basingstoke. Timothy came along, too, but he was now about fourteen years old. One way of reckoning a cat's age compared with our own is to count one for the first year and then six years for every one thereafter. As a rough-and-ready comparison it is not bad. A cat aged fourteen is the equivalent of a man aged seventy-nine, which is probably about right. Timothy had lived an active life but when he was fourteen he was certainly showing his age. Our move, too, deprived him of the undisturbed solitude to which he had become accustomed. However, he had a large garden, with some rough ground included, in which to hunt for shrews and doze away the sunny days. He was approaching his fifteenth birthday when he went into a rapid decline and, on the recommendation of the vet, we had him put down.

At this time my wife had two grey cats, mother and daughter. Both had beauty but lacked personality. I never tried but I suspect it would have been difficult, if not impossible, to teach them anything, even the simplest words of command. Cats, like dogs, vary greatly in intelligence but most of them can be made to understand and obey certain simple words of command. Cats, of course, will never appreciate word-meanings as we do (and the same applies to dogs) and it is pathetic to listen to cat-owners sometimes talking to their cats as if they were highly intelligent human-beings capable of weighing up every word. If a young cat is trying to sharpen its claws at the expense of an upholstered chair or sofa it is really quite useless to attempt to upbraid it by saying: 'Fluffles, you must not do that!' Cats, in my experience, react most quickly to the tone of voice and the simplicity of any command. A really irascible 'Stop it', will arrest any cat in mid-air, so to speak, although it may have to be repeated in the early stages of tuition. I have managed to get most of my cats to understand what I mean by the command 'No' if they show signs of doing something which you do not propose to allow them to do, and 'Out!' if they have ventured into the larder or any other forbidden place. If rapped out smartly most cats soon learn that you mean what you say. It is as much the tone of your voice as the word itself which conveys the message and it is just as simple to get an adult cat to understand that you are pleased with it if you address it in honeyed tones and your pleasure can be further emphasized by tickling the cat under the chin or by stroking it. But your displeasure should depend upon the ugly, sharp tone of your address and never on hitting the creature.

I had derived a good deal of pleasure from Timothy and

he had certainly converted me to ginger cats. However, when he died I did not feel any particular urge to effect a replacement which, I suppose, shows that I really was far from being a cat-lover. If it would be true to say that I missed him, it would probably be equally true to say that I got along quite well without him. It was sheer chance, not choice, which brought the next ginger cat into our household.

One October evening, a year or two after the passing of ginger Tim, I had got back from my London office and was sitting down to supper when my wife informed me that neighbours had reported a small ginger cat that was, they said, 'lost'. I had my doubts as to whether this story was correct but, in any event, as there was not the slightest chance of finding even a lost cat in the dark, I finished my meal and had settled down to smoke a pipe over a cup of coffee, when the door-bell rang and my wife went to answer it. I could just catch the voices without being able to decipher the conversation but as the strange voice was a soprano I assumed that my spouse was having a passing crack with one of her buddies. However, when the chatter had gone on for several minutes my curiosity got the better of me and I went out to investigate. The visitor, however, was a stranger to me so I went into the kitchen and, switching on the light, spied a small beautifully marked ginger cat. My wife had peeled some potatoes for our meal and had put the peelings in an old saucepan and placed the pan under the kitchen table prior to disposing of the contents. The cat was eating these wretched peelings as if they were caviare. It was not frightened when I seized the saucepan but followed me round, somewhat dismayed, I think, at this sudden removal of the food, because it was nearly starved. It made no fuss when I picked it up, discovering in the process that it was little more than a bag of bones. His coat, however, was in good condition and he was obviously a youngster, probably not more than a year old. We both 'clicked' from the start and as soon as he had got some good food inside him he marched about the house as if he owned the whole place and then came and sat down with us by the fireside as if he had been doing the same thing for months. I have never known a cat so tame or so adaptable and he became a welcome member of the household.

I made a cat-ladder so that the newcomer, which I named Belmonte, could come in via our bedroom window if he were out after dark and to enable him to get out before we rose in the morning if he wished to do so. He was with us for eight or nine months. Then, early one summer's morning, when it was only just light, I saw him leap to the window-sill and disappear via the cat-ladder. He never returned and we never discovered what had happened to him in spite of a good deal of searching and extensive enquiries. If one knows that a cat or dog has been run over or killed in some way it is far better than not knowing what has happened to it. It may be stupid but on occasions like the mysterious disappearance of Belmonte imagination is apt to run riot, so that one pictures the cat accidentally shut up perhaps in some garage or outbuilding and starving to death. I really was upset at the loss of this engaging young creature but it was my wife who decided that he must be replaced.

In the following September she announced that on one of her brother's farms there was a charming ginger kitten which would be put down unless we took it in. So we had another ginger cat, not particularly elegant (he had very short legs) and not nearly so well marked as either Timothy or Belmonte had been. I regarded him as a bit of a peasant in the feline world which, I suppose, is the reason why I gave him the rather absurd name of Billy Williams. He was a proper rustic, full of high spirits but, even for a kitten, decidedly slow in the uptake. He gave us a lot of fun throughout the winter and then in the spring was cut off in his prime when he was run over and instantly killed by a passing car. The road outside our house had originally been a lane running between steep banks on either side and it was not to be long before I realized that this was something of a death-trap for any high-spirited kitten which had not yet learned any roadsense. At least we knew that Billy Williams could hardly have known what had hit him. I buried him in the orchard and that, so far as I was concerned, was the end of our saga of marmalade cats. We had, after all, lost two of them within a twelve-month.

Two months later I was in our local inn when a chap came up to me and said that he understood I had recently lost a ginger cat and that I wanted another one. I thanked him but declined the offer with what I regarded as sensible firmness. But it so happened that this fellow was a farm-hand and he went on to tell me that it was a pity that I did not want the cat because they had a litter of kittens on the farm and one of them was a magnificent creature, as wild as they come. He explained that he did not like cats himself but he thought that this particular kitten was so big for its age that it would develop into an outstanding cat. Shrugging his shoulders, he said that if I did not want it then this ginger cat would have to be put down along with his brothers and sisters.

I was intrigued with his description of the kitten and I suppose that I was also weak-minded. However, I played for time to the extent that I said I would ask my wife, yet I knew full well that, far from raising any objections, she would be all in favour of introducing this potential giant into the household. I met the chap in the pub that evening and told him that I would come over on a bicycle plus a basket at midday on the Sunday. I cycled over and brought the kitten back. It was certainly large for an eight-week-old but it was not so much a tabby-ginger as a plain sandy with faint brown stripes. It was, however, a beautifully proportioned cat and we gave him the impressive name of Johnny Culachy of Rymore, although we always called him Culachy for short, except when we wanted to impress strangers. Only a few weeks after we had acquired Culachy my wife bowled me over by announcing one evening that we were about to become the owners of yet another ginger kitten. Before I could raise any sort of protest she added that it would be very desirable for Johnny Culachy to have a companion. Two kittens, playing together, she said, would ease the burden of our having to try to entertain one on its own. The new kitten duly arrived at the end of August when it was six or seven weeks old. I admit that I fell for him from the outset and I called him Uncle Whiskers after the name of a racehorse which was running rather well in that year of 1959.

Uncle Whiskers

I

From the moment of his arrival as a very small kitten it was obvious that Uncle Whiskers would develop into a very handsome cat. He was what you might call sharp-featured, with a rather pointed face and small ears. His body and limbs were beautifully proportioned and his only obvious defect, not a serious one, was that his tail was a bit on the 'thin' side. Even as a small kitten, however, it was impossible to fault his colour-scheme – a rich, almost glowing orange-brown on a base of golden sand. He was lavishly striped and mottled, too, and the pattern was delightfully symmetrical. He was short-furred, too, which to my way of thinking is always an advantage. So, even as a kitten, he 'showed promise' as they say, but cats in the kitten stage all rather tend to be much of a muchness, high-spirited and mischievous but with most of their own peculiar characteristics either still latent or scarcely developed.

None the less, Uncle Whiskers was an exceptional cat. I believe that, in the course of time, he became a unique one. It would be pleasant to suggest that he was a quite exceptional small kitten but, looking back, I doubt if this was true. Neither he nor Johnny Culachy had any evil in them, but they both possessed needle-sharp claws that could be made to feel more than painful whenever either one decided to use you as a sort of indoor tree by climbing up your legs and eventually lodging on your shoulder. Both of them had to be weaned out of the costly and objectionable habit of using the upholstered backs of chairs, carpets or even wallpaper as excellent objects for sharpening their claws. In the case of kittens, in my experience, this can only be done by intervening at once, picking the offender up by the scruff of the neck, showing your grave displeasure by prolonged, growling rebukes and, if the subject doesn't even then appear to be properly deflated, blowing in his face . . . and if he then has the cheek to spit at you, spit back at him, for with a bit of practice it is possible to make some ugly sucking and hissing noises through tightly-clenched teeth.

We were lucky, in that winter of 1959–60, to have two kittens of much the same age, for single kittens can be somewhat demanding on one's time. Between mercifully frequent intervals of sleeping, they simply must exercise their young limbs and work off the boundless energy with which most of them are naturally endowed. Like most puppies, they greatly enjoy a mock fight, but the best and most labour-saving device to keep a kitten amused when it is indoors is a fair supply of ping-pong balls. These are light and bouncy and any young feline will be happy to chase one round and round the room or up and down the passage until, utterly exhausted, it curls up and goes to sleep. All you have to do then is to find the ping-pong ball. This will probably involve you in a lot of stooping so that you may peer hopefully underneath this bit of furniture or that. However, it is all very good exercise, even if you may not always appreciate that fact at the time.

Uncle Whiskers and Johnny Culachy spent most of their waking hours amusing one another, either indoors or out. They would indulge in endless chases, intermixed with spells of what one might call high-spirited gambolling, racing up and down the stairs, in and out of the rooms and along the passages. Johnny Culachy, as I have said, was built on the big side. He was also at least two months older than Uncle Whiskers. In their fun and games, therefore, he was by far the stronger cat of the two. But if Uncle Whiskers was outmatched in what one might call the in-fighting, he scored all the points at long range. Although much smaller, he was quicker over the sprint distances than Johnny Culachy and in trying to escape his pursuer he gave us the first glimpses of the extraordinary intelligence he developed in adult life. He kept on changing his various hiding-places. Johnny Culachy was, perhaps, a bit dim-witted, almost invariably investigating those hide-outs that were either most conspicuous or nearest to the point of his entry into any room. Thus Uncle Whiskers might have ensconced himself on the seat of a chair pushed under the dining-table. His pursuer would enter, silently and cautiously, then move gingerly to the sideboard, beneath which he would then peer with obvious excitement, pushing his head and neck well underneath the piece of furniture as if he was certain his quarry *must* be there. His opponent took this grand opportunity to take a flying leap at him, thus catching him at a grave disadvantage. By the time Johnny Culachy had managed to extricate him-self Uncle Whiskers would be scampering away up the stairs to safety.

These amiable larks might continue for an hour or more. They were both amusing and highly diverting and if, occasionally, you were very tired and imagined that the antics of the kittens were getting on your nerves, you could shut yourself in a room and leave them to get on with their games, which they were able to do very well in your self-imposed absence. With an intelligent adult cat it is possible, given patience and experience, to get it to enter, to some extent, into your world. You may even, if you try hard enough, be able to enter into a very small part of a cat's world, although very often people actually believe that they are doing this when, in fact, they are simply being very childish. But the world of a kitten is almost impenetrable and you must rest content, mostly, to play the role of a spectator. Unless you are tragically handicapped by the lack of any sense of humour you should be able to enjoy yourself.

Johnny Culachy and Uncle Whiskers, both growing apace, certainly had fun all through their first winter and, with the prospect of their growing out of kittenhood into a couple of good feline characters, the future seemed rosy enough. Culachy was a big, beautifully proportioned cat already. Uncle Whiskers more than made up for his smaller size by the richness of his colouring and, for a kitten, his already outstanding IQ.

Early in the March of 1960 I had been away on business over a week-end and when I arrived back in my office on the Monday I heard the disastrous news that I had lost yet another cat. Johnny Culachy of Rymore had been hit by a car whilst crossing the road and instantly killed. My wife had left me to act as undertaker and when I got home in the evening I went into the outhouse with a torch and looked at this splendid creature laid out on a shelf. Apart from a dribble of coagulated blood around the mouth, he looked almost as noble in death as he had done in life. It seemed a shame that he had been cut off almost at the beginning of things but nothing in life is more final than death and there was nothing left to do but to bury him, so I rose early in the morning, dug a hole in the orchard and laid Johnny Culachy to rest. As I shovelled the earth over him I made a silent vow that I would never have another kitten at that house unless it was a stray, like Belmonte. The embanked lane was a death-trap for young cats.

It is not easy to assess to what extent one cat may miss another one. Uncle Whiskers and Johnny Culachy had been wonderful buddies for several months, yet I rather doubt if cats are capable of feeling any sadness on occasions like these, simply because they cannot possibly appreciate what may have happened to a vanished companion. But that they 'miss' such a companion, at any rate for some days or even a week or two, I would think to be a fact beyond dispute. Certainly Uncle Whiskers displayed every evidence of being both puzzled and frustrated. For days he would hunt about the house in the evening, obviously looking for a game with Johnny Culachy and only after a long search would he finally come and sit, somewhat disconsolately we thought, in front of the fire.

When Billy Williams had been a kitten I had purchased two ping-pong balls and on the long winter evenings I had given both the cat and myself a good deal of fun by standing at the foot of the stairs with the kitten beside me and then throwing the ping-pong ball up to the top of the flight. The cat would race up the stairs and, with a bit of luck, just as he arrived at the top of the stairs the ball would bounce back off the wall and come plop-plopping down, bouncing from tread to tread with the cat, who had done a smart about-turn, chasing after it. A few minutes of this high-speed fun soon worked-off the kitten's high spirits.

So I used the ping-pong ball in this way to try to provide Uncle Whiskers with at least some sort of a substitute for the fun and games that he had enjoyed in the evenings with Johnny Culachy. Cats are usually regarded as very independent creatures and, compared with dogs, most of which are very dependent, this is probably true. But most cats are independent, in my view, because of the attitude of their owners, many of whom treat them in a very casual and off-hand way once the initial novelty of ownership has worn off. When some people tell me that their cat is 'no bother' I suspect that what some of them really mean is that they don't bother about the cat. It isn't much bother, for instance, to kick a cat out into a wet winter's night and shut it out until such time as you may choose to get up next morning to let it in for breakfast but in such circumstances the animal hasn't got any option except to be independent.

When I arrived home in the evenings I used to have my supper and then I always gave Uncle Whiskers ten minutes of high-jinks with the ping-pong ball. Young as he was, he soon got used to the routine, sitting expectantly throughout the meal. As soon as I went to the sideboard and took the ball out of a fruit-bowl he became wide-eyed with excitement, anticipating the fun by dashing off to the foot of the stairs. He would wait, pent-up with eagerness, every muscle tensed, until he saw my arm go forward prior to throwing the ball and then he would bound up like a rocket. Sometimes, to fool him, I didn't release the ball but he was remarkably quick in the uptake and, seeing no ball, would put the brakes on in mid-flight, turning round to stare at me. I only had to show him that I still had the ping-pong ball in my hand and he would come scampering back to the starting-point. I gave him a lot of fun but certainly not more fun than he gave me!

However, the spring was coming on and the days were lengthening and Uncle Whiskers spent most of the daytime in the garden and sometimes a part of the evenings as well. If it was a wet or windy evening he would soon tap on the french windows of the sitting-room to be re-admitted but if the weather was fine, especially so if there was moonlight, he might stop out for hours, using the cat-ladder up to our bedroom window (always left open) to rejoin us at whatever time suited his purpose. He was an extremely quiet cat and we seldom heard him either coming up the ladder or entering the room, so that it was usually not until we woke up in the morning to find him curled up, asleep, on the end of the bed that we were aware of his safe return from a night's hunting.

During that summer of 1960 – the first complete summer

of his life – Uncle Whiskers began to spend much of the day sleeping, either in some favourite hidy-hole in the long grasses if the weather was fine or, if it was raining, in what we rather ostentatiously called the summerhouse, which was really little more than a large, windproof wooden shed which we had opened up on its southern or sunny side. Uncle Whiskers usually got active around teatime but it was not until sunset that his hunting instincts were really roused. He would then sit patiently amid the tall, rough grasses of the orchard, ever on the alert for shrews. He often pounced but the cover was too thick. On warm, still evenings when there were plenty of moths flitting around in the gloaming he would be on parade on the lawn, leaping up and attempting, usually unsuccessfully, to claw down an insect flickering above him. He was growing up apace and there could be little doubt that he was enjoying life to the full. He had grown out of post-prandial larks with a ping-pong ball. I was really rather sorry!

II

It was a golden day towards the end of September of that indifferent summer of 1960. My wife and I were having tea together in our sitting-room. It was both warm and windless, one of those precious days of early autumn which really belong to summer. The french windows were open on to the lawn, the borders bright with michaelmas daisies, dahlias and other flowers of autumn. Swallows and martins were hawking flies against a background of lucid blue sky. It was a heavenly Saturday afternoon.

The peace and tranquillity were suddenly broken by abrupt knocking on our back-door. My wife went out into the kitchen. I followed her. Two youths, one as white as a sheet, were asking my wife if we had a ginger cat. When my wife admitted that we had one of the youths informed us that they had just run over it with their van.

I heard my wife explaining that Uncle Whiskers had been indoors with us only two or three minutes before. It could not, she felt, be him. I was not so sure. I knew of no other ginger cat in the immediate vicinity. In any case, if they had rammed a cat it was necessary to discover the victim without delay.

I found drops of fresh blood in the road outside the house. I followed the trail through a high thorn hedge into what we grandiosely called the orchard. It was more difficult to follow the trail of bright red spots through the thick, rank grasses between the apple trees; it might have been almost impossible had it not been that the red trail was becoming ominously more obvious in so far as more blood was being dropped. Then, thirty yards from the scene of the accident, I came across Uncle Whiskers lying on his side, his richly-marked ginger fur gleaming with blotches of ugly red smears. He was in a dazed, almost unconscious state and did not even prick his ears in answer to his name.

I picked the luckless creature up as carefully as I could. Uncle Whiskers was not yet dead but the pupils of his eyes were widely dilated. His mouth, from which a trickle of blood was oozing, was wide open and he was panting for breath. His left front leg was smashed almost to smithereens, broken in many places, with splintered bones showing through the torn flesh and fur.

I knew it was a hopeless case. All I could do was to rush the dying creature to my admirable vet in the nearby town and have him destroyed as soon as possible. I felt sick at heart and there was no comfort now in the mellow, autumnal sunshine and the excited twitterings of young house-martins being fed in their nest of mud under the eaves of the house.

One of the two young men drove me, at good speed, over

the three miles into town. I had a bath-towel folded thickly across my knees and held the cat on that. The bleeding had, perhaps, eased a little but Uncle Whiskers was gasping for breath with jaws wide open. I could not be sure, but my impression was that he was almost unconscious. Over the last half of this desperate journey I began to wonder if the services of the vet would be needed.

Veterinary surgeons, in my long experience, are a remarkable and devoted breed. In this particular one, whom I had known for many years, I had complete confidence. He came at once from his own tea-table into the surgery and I was mightily relieved to know that he would waste no time in putting Uncle Whiskers out of his agony. He went over the cat pretty thoroughly and then said: 'It's a young cat, isn't it?'

'Just over a year old,' I replied.

'Nice cat. I could amputate this smashed leg completely and sew in the stump. His other front leg seems a bit gammy but it's not broken. The rest of him seems okay but he may have internal injuries. You want me to put him down?'

I was momentarily nonplussed. The very notion of not having the cat destroyed had not occurred to me.

'You're the expert,' I said. 'I just don't want the cat to suffer but if you think there's even a chance of saving him I don't care what I spend. But I want him to live a happy life, not a half-baked one.'

'I can't really say at the moment. I can't promise anything until I've got this shattered leg off and we can see whether there's anything else wrong. I wouldn't be too hopeful if I were you.'

Too hopeful? My heart came out of my boots at the very notion that there might be even an outside chance of a reprieve. 'Please have a go,' I urged. 'But I give you a free hand to put him down if you think that's best. Shall I ring you tomorrow to find out how things are going?'

'Yes,' replied the vet. 'Ring about one o'clock.'

Anxious to impress upon my friendly vet that he was not dealing with a Fluffy or a Tiddles or any ordinary, run-of-the-mill cat, I said on parting: 'His name is Uncle Whiskers.' Was it imagination or did the tip of the tail of that shattered hulk twitch, be it ever so feebly, in answer to his name?

That was the first night for more than a year that Uncle Whiskers did not sleep on our bed, tucked in against my feet. I didn't sleep soundly, either, for wondering whether Uncle Whiskers was already dead or whether he was alive and, if so, how much alive? What sort of a life could be lived by a three-legged cat, anyway? In my night-long anxiety I probably underestimated the vet. I certainly underestimated Uncle Whiskers.

III

If I slept at all that night it was no more than a doze. I remembered a terrier that had done famously on three legs, so perhaps Uncle Whiskers would be all right on three legs. Yet how absurd it was to be worrying about a cat, even if he was a bit of a charmer. I had, after all, spent most of my life without a cat. Anyway, Uncle Whiskers had probably been put down hours ago, so worrying was an idle business. I went on tossing and turning until daybreak, which I suppose was exceedingly stupid. I would not know the worst until the middle of the next day, anyway.

That particular Sunday was another gloriously fine day, but the sunshine failed to pierce my gloom. The morning dragged on. Maybe it was wholly irrational to be temporarily almost obsessed over the welfare of a cat but I can only recall the facts. I simply could not settle to anything. I longed for one o'clock to arrive, so that I could telephone the vet as arranged. And no sooner did I want that hour to arrive than I funked it. I would only learn that Uncle Whiskers had been destroyed and that I would never see him again.

I decided to bicycle down to our local inn at noon, a distance of a mile. Though I am not a man of great courage, I am not a coward, either. But I am bound to admit that on that morning I was in something akin to a blue-funk, unwilling to face up to what I knew would prove the reality. So I sought relief in what, at its highest level, was no better than a form of rather childish escapism.

I went to the inn and drank with my friends and, to screw up my courage to face the ordeal at one o'clock, I am fairly certain that I imbibed more freely than usual. I would like to be able to record that at that vital hour I marched resolutely to the telephone, head held high, inserted my two pennies, dialled the vet's number and generally comported myself like an officer and a gentleman. In fact, for want of a better analogy, I dragged my feet to that public telephone in much the same mood as, many years before, I had approached my headmaster's study to receive a caning. If there were no butterflies in my stomach then they must have been moths.

I dialled the number and listened to the buzz-buzz. Uncle Whiskers was dead? Uncle Whiskers was doing fine? Uncle Whiskers was in a bad way? Why didn't the confounded vet answer? Then I heard the click as the receiver came off; I pressed button A and felt my heart sink into my boots. This was it!

'Hello.'

'This is Philip Brown.'

'You're enquiring about your cat?' (Why couldn't he tell me, straight away, that Uncle Whiskers had been put down?) 'I had no difficulty with the amputation. I took the whole leg off and stitched up the stump. That's all gone fine but I'm not sure about the other front leg at the moment, though it isn't broken, that's sure.'

'What's wrong with the other leg?' I asked, horrified with a vision of a young cat without any front legs.

'I can't say at the moment. We must wait and see.'

'But the cat's all right?'

'He's been awfully badly knocked about, I'm afraid, but considering his injuries, he's doing very well. I think he may be all right.'

'How long will you want to keep him?'

'About a week. Unless I let you know, expect him back next Saturday evening.'

'We'll be in next Saturday – and I'm grateful for what you've done. Of course you have a free hand to put him down if you think fit.'

'I shan't have to put him down. He's a young kitten and full of guts. Considering his bashing he's in remarkable shape. You'll see him next Saturday, I hope.'

I cycled home, perhaps a trifle light-headed but with a song in my heart, the latter organ having come back out of my boots with remarkable speed. Uncle Whiskers was not dead, although I still did not appreciate how lucky I was that he was still alive. I think that if I had been asked at the time why I was so anxious about this young ginger cat I might have found it difficult to provide a convincing answer. I had, however, never had the good fortune to watch any of my 'marmaladers' grow to maturity. Belmonte could not have been above two years old when he disappeared; Billy Williams and Johnny Culachy had both been killed in their first year; even ginger Timothy, although he had lived to a ripe old age and died a natural death, had been largely denied to me over the first half of his life because of war service. So if ever I was to watch a cat grow up a great deal depended on the survival of Uncle Whiskers. It was also true he was one of the most beautifully marked cats I had ever known and had already displayed intelligence far above the average for a very young cat.

Once or twice during the week following the accident I rang the vet and was relieved to learn that the condition of the patient was 'satisfactory'. On the Saturday evening I was agog with suppressed excitement, waiting for Uncle Whiskers to be restored to us. Just as twilight was starting to gather and my wife and I were thinking about our suppers, there was a knock at the door. It was the vet, carrying a wicker basket in which Uncle Whiskers was hidden. He came through to the sitting-room and placed the basket on the rug in front of a fire that we had just kindled. All that I had to do now was to slide out the securing-rod and welcome Uncle Whiskers, a golden charmer missing one front leg, back into the fold. At this triumphant moment there ought to have been a fanfare of trumpets . . .

Crouching at the bottom of the basket was a cat. But it was not the sleek, confident creature with glowing orange markings that I had remembered. It looked, and indeed it was, the wreck of a young cat. He allowed me to lift him out and place him on the rug without a murmur or a gesture of protest but he behaved as if he were still in a daze. There were eleven stitches in the wound resulting from the amputation of his left leg but it was clearly healing well. The other front leg seemed limp and lifeless, the foot twisted round grotesquely upon itself. Apart from the general tattiness of his fur, the rest of him seemed to be all right. But what, I wondered in genuine horror, would be the use of two excellent hind legs with one front leg missing completely and the other, so far as one could see, not much better than a useless impediment? The cat had sunk down on his chest and chin, thus making his hindquarters appear raised up at a most awkward and unfeline angle.

Unfortunately the vet could offer little encouragement about the remaining front limb. As a result of the accident the nerves had been severed and there was a radial paralysis. This might well be permanent. On the other hand there might be a partial – just conceivably an almost complete – recovery of the use of this vital limb. Time alone would tell. Apart from all this the vet was satisfied that the cat was in good physical condition and certainly not suffering any pain. He promised to look in again in a week's time to remove the stitches. I thanked him as he took his leave, convinced that he had performed a miracle for no good purpose whatsoever.

My wife went to the kitchen to prepare our meal and some choice delicacies for the invalid. I returned to the sitting-room, sat on a chair and stared at the shattered creature huddled forlornly on the rug. And the longer I stared at Uncle Whiskers the more horrified I felt. If that one remaining front paw failed to mend then, through my own selfishness, I would surely have doomed him to a life of frustration. It seemed to me that, unless that damaged limb mended considerably, the future life of Uncle Whiskers was likely to be little better than a sort of living death. Many times during the next few days I cursed myself for a rogue and a fool for not insisting that the vet should put the cat down in the first place. But vets should know; I could only console myself with the knowledge that I had accepted the vet's advice.

After a few minutes I called Uncle Whiskers by name. His tail flicked in response but he made no attempt to look round. This was an encouraging sign, so I got down on the floor and stroked his matted, dishevelled fur. Uncle Whiskers began to purr, very softly. Suddenly, with a sort of convulsive push with his back legs he tumbled awkwardly on to his side. I tickled his tummy as he gazed at me with his orange-yellow eyes. Then he stretched out his back legs to their fullest extent and his purring developed into a roar of pleasure. This was a good sign and my flagging spirits rose.

My wife called from the kitchen that Uncle Whiskers' supper was ready. Should we bring the plate of meat and the saucerful of creamy milk and give them to him on the rug or should we see if he could make any progress towards the kitchen? Sooner or later Uncle Whiskers would have to try to become mobile again, however awkward, slow and laborious his movements might be. So my wife clinked the plate with a fork, which had always been the signal for feeding time and Uncle Whiskers, obviously hungry and eager, somehow got on to his hind legs, bottom in the air and his tail stuck up straight above it, but with his chin and chest on the rug. He tried to move forward by shoving with his hind legs and immediately tumbled over himself in a most undignified way. He lurched into action again, only to collapse once more. At the end of each mighty effort he finished up facing in a different direction but he made no forward progress whatsoever. It was a sickening performance to watch. Frustrated, bewildered and exhausted, he finally crouched down on the rug and gave voice to one of the most plaintive mews he had ever uttered.

So we brought his food to him but he had great difficulty in even raising his head high enough to get over the edge of the platter. However, he scoffed the meat with evident relish. He found even greater difficulty in tackling the milk, soaking the fur beneath his chin in the process but, in his own good time, he got most of it inside him. I could, perhaps, have assisted him but it seemed to me that he would have to learn to do things for himself. After finishing the milk he made an awkward, half-hearted attempt to wash himself, then tumbled over on his side and started to worry at the stitches in his long scar with his teeth. He still seemed to have a fair amount of strength but at last he wearied of his futile efforts, falling fast asleep in front of the wood fire.

At the end of the evening we carried him upstairs to our bedroom and tucked him up on an old eiderdown on the floor. We would have put him on a chair or even on the bed but we were frightened that he might fall off. With only two hind legs, what might happen if he were to fall only a foot or two on to a hard and unyielding surface? He hardly opened his eyes during the move but when we snugged him down for the night he sang softly for a minute or two before falling asleep again. He was still sleeping soundly when we woke up on the following morning.

IV

If Uncle Whiskers was bewildered and baffled by the turn of events which had changed him, almost overnight, from a whole and active cat into less than half a cat and sorely crippled at that, let me admit that I, too, was bewildered and baffled. It was all very well to ask oneself whether or not one had done the right thing in not insisting that the horribly maimed creature should be destroyed, but the die had been cast. Uncle Whiskers, whatever his plight, was very much alive. True, he had lost one leg completely and the remaining front one was, at the moment, as useless for any kind of locomotion as the missing limb, but the rest of him, as they say, was bonny enough, yet all he could achieve by thrusting with his mobile hind legs was to tumble over himself in a most undignified and frustrating way. What made it so irksome to watch his vain efforts was that Uncle Whiskers simply could not understand why they failed to work.

The pressing problem was to decide how we were going

to surmount the difficulties at least sufficiently well to ensure that the unlucky cat could enjoy a reasonably full and happy life – and it had to be a question of 'we', for although I was confident that I would be able to help Uncle Whiskers on his road to recovery, very much was bound to depend upon the cat himself. Most cats can be independent when they choose. The accident had rendered Uncle Whiskers, at least for the time being, very much dependent. Any recovery to normal was bound to be slow; I was not too optimistic that Uncle Whiskers could ever live anything like a full life again. But it was a challenge that would require close relationship with the cat and a good deal of trust, if not actual faith, by both parties if there were to be any prospect of a tolerably successful outcome. Probably for the first time in my life I felt some genuine affinity to a cat. The very fact that we were, so to speak, in the job together made something of a compact between us. It was a challenge, anyway, so far as I was concerned and life would be boring without its difficulties and problems.

During the first week following Uncle Whiskers' return from the vet, however, I did little about the challenge beyond a good deal of serious pondering and watching the cat. Uncle Whiskers was, for the present, immobile. So he had to have his food brought to him; he had to be carried to and from his earth-box to relieve the calls of nature (which he did not like at all, for he had always been allowed to go outdoors to perform these essentially private functions) and had to be carried up to our bedroom each night and down again in the morning. He did something to relieve the tedium of his restricted life by washing himself. He was a slim, lissom cat and he became visibly more and more elastic as the days passed. One evening, only a few days after his return, whilst lounging on the rug by the fireside he suddenly surprised us by raising himself on his hind legs, his tail stuck straight out behind him as a sort of third leg, stretching himself upwards and upwards, the paralysed front paw drooping down across his chest and the stump of the amputated leg visibly moving beneath the stitched scar. This movement ended in a somewhat ignominious collapse but it was, in embryo form, the start of one of his greatest and unique performances – the ability to sit upright on his haunches for minutes on end, looking around and taking notice of all that might be going on around him. Yet all that was in the future, unknown to us then; he was still incapable of making any co-ordinated progress in moving in any direction whatsoever.

Before the vet returned at the end of the week Uncle Whiskers successfully resolved one problem, that of washing his face. Cats wash their faces by licking a front paw, then rubbing it over their faces and around their ears, repeating the process until that part of their toilet is completed. Unfortunately Uncle Whiskers had no use whatsoever in his only remaining front paw. He could not even direct it to his mouth, let alone wash over his face with it. So he resolved this difficulty by licking the paw as it lay, crumpled back on itself, on the ground, after which he vigorously rubbed his face on it. It was not the approved feline method but it was equally effective, all the same, and very soon his appearance was as clean and spruce as it had ever been.

When the vet returned to remove the stitches at which Uncle Whiskers had bitten and worried in vain for a week, the cat looked in much better fettle than at any time since the accident a fortnight earlier. He not only did not object to the whipping-out of the stitches but was actually purring with delight before the job was done. The vet expressed great satisfaction with his general condition but was more dubious about the state of the remaining front leg, on which I felt that the mobility of the cat must ultimately depend.

The nerves had been severed, there was a radial paralysis and the vet was highly doubtful as to whether it could ever serve him as a third leg. I was a bit depressed but Uncle Whiskers went on singing his heart out and then repeated, his 'sitting-up' trick, balancing himself more securely this time, moving his head to look this way and that, purring away with merriment. At least he was no ordinary cat. I knew that the vet had done a remarkable job and he was clearly pleased that the cat had not been put down. I admit that I felt rather less confident about the future. Even if Uncle Whiskers was, more or less, fit and well, he surely could not enjoy the many years of life that, with luck, lay ahead of him if he were virtually incapable of moving away from any spot where we might set him down.

I realized at the outset that only Uncle Whiskers himself could strive to overcome this handicap of immobility. What I had to do was to try to encourage him to make the effort, however painful and possibly futile it might be for both of us. So my wife and I decided that, whilst we would carry him about the house as required throughout much of the day, bringing him his breakfast and light luncheon in the dining-room, we would call him to his dinner in the kitchen. If, within a reasonable time, he did not succeed in making much progress towards his objective then we would carry him the rest of the way but, each succeeding day, we resolved that he must do better than on the preceding one.

It was, by any standards, a pitiable performance to watch. Although he seemed to be steadily gaining strength in his already powerful hind limbs, Uncle Whiskers could achieve little or nothing with his paralysed front leg, spending most of his time stumbling over himself, sometimes still turning a complete somersault, ending up by facing in entirely the wrong direction to that in which he was desperately trying to go. But he persisted with a gameness that was admirable and although, at first, he would take ten minutes to cover a yard (at the end of which time we just could not stand it any longer and gave him a lift to his journey's end) at the end of a week or two he succeeded, however slowly and laboriously, in covering the half-dozen yards into the kitchen and the feasting.

It was during this early period of his rehabilitation that Uncle Whiskers soon became really adept at sitting upright on his hind legs. In point of fact, much of his forward progress, in those early days, consisted of sitting upright on his haunches, stretching himself up to his fullest extent (some two feet) and then diving forward in the direction he wanted to go. He would then shuffle his hind legs up until they were almost under his chin so that he was bent in a sort of tight bow-shape, whereupon he would sit up, stretch again and dive forward. Slow he might be, but Uncle Whiskers soon got over the initial clumsiness of this new sort of locomotion. Within two or three weeks, if he wanted to get somewhere 'on the flat', he would make his goal in his own good time.

One evening when we had had our own meal and then called him into the kitchen for his whilst we were doing the washing-up, we left Uncle Whiskers lapping away at a saucerful of milk. As far as I remember we were watching a programme on television. The cat did not come back into the dining-room but we were not worried, feeling that he was content enough, probably washing himself, and would return to the fireside when he chose to do so. But when we switched off the television he was still missing, so I went out to the kitchen. Uncle Whiskers was not there. So a search was organized and we eventually found him, curled up and fast asleep, on the end of our bed. He had managed not only to get along the hall to the foot of the stairs but had then surmounted all seventeen treads, had moved into the bedroom and finally leapt on to the bed unaided. It was a

November night to remember! I woke him up, stroking him and making congratulatory noises. Uncle Whiskers was delighted, purring away like a rattling nightjar and rolling about in an ecstasy. So far as he was concerned, he conveyed the impression that there was nothing much wrong with the world!

Two things were rapidly becoming clear. The first was a somewhat depressing one. There could now be little doubt that the cat's sole remaining front leg was going to remain pretty useless. He had no feeling in it and no muscular control over it, either at the elbow or the wrist; the hand (I suppose one ought to call it the front foot) was uselessly and rather grotesquely turned over on itself and he was incapable of extending or retracting any of the claws. Nor was he able to sharpen the claws against the bark of a tree, as most cats do, so that it became necessary to cut the claws back about once a fortnight with a pair of nail-clippers. It was his habit, as soon as the claws grew long, to start biting them vigorously with his very sharp teeth, which was always a reminder to get the clippers out. He never objected to having his claws cut; on the contrary, he lay over on his back and usually began purring the moment one started on this simple task.

The front limb, however, was not *wholly* useless. The muscles of the shoulder and part of the upper 'arm' were still intact and as strong as ever. There was hope to be got from the fact that Uncle Whiskers soon started to attempt to use this limb from the shoulder, first pushing down on it in order to raise his chest clear of the ground and then immediately 'throwing' it forward as far as possible. He then half-pulled himself forward, relying on waddling on his back legs to complete the effort. Once he had discovered his ability to move in this manner he began to make rapid progress. He suddenly learnt that, by this means, he could go up a flight of stairs even more rapidly than he could move forward on level ground. So, to hasten his rehabilitation by exercising his muscles and helping him to co-ordinate his movements, I used to get out a ping-pong ball in the evenings. Taking both the ball and the cat to the foot of the stairs. I would then take the ping-pong ball and toss it up the stairs, gently enough to ensure that, nine times out of ten, it did not rebound from the wall at the top and come plop-plopping back down the stairs.

The moment he saw me throw the ball Uncle Whiskers scampered up the stairs after it as fast as he could go. On reaching the landing at the top he would scuffle about with the ball until, sooner or later, it came bouncing down. He followed its descent in spirit, peering wide-eyed over the topmost tread, his head nodding up and down as he watched the flight of the ball. Then I had to carry him down and restart the fun and games. He never tired of it, but after a long day in the office I did. However, it was rewarding to see how rapidly he developed the use of his hind legs and the strength of his muscles, not to mention at least some sort of rudimentary co-ordination between that almost useless front flipper and the rest of him.

These evening games went well until, one day, he attempted to descend the stairs as the ping-pong ball bounced downwards. He fell with his chest on the top tread, paused to get his balance, then brought his back legs down, rather awkwardly and with a crab-wise shuffle of the body, with a little skip and jump. He then repeated the performance, step after careful step, until he finally arrived at the foot of the stairs at his very first attempt. He then leapt on the elusive ping-pong ball, sent it flying and plodded after it.

By Christmas, only three months after his accident, Uncle Whiskers was able to get about the house at will, upstairs or down, even if his progress was slow compared with that of a normal cat – especially so if he was descending. His magnificent coat of fur had completely recovered its pristine glory, his stripes a rich, glowing orange and a healthy sheen on every hair. He had very soon learnt to groom himself perfectly, having plenty of time on his paws, so to speak, which more than made up for any slowness in his toiletry. Better still, he had now learnt to make use of his one remaining front leg to wash his face in the approved feline fashion. He no longer had recourse to first licking the paw and then rubbing his face against it, for now he had at least a little use of the shoulder muscles on that side. So he sat upright on his strong haunches, tail stretched out rigidly behind him to ensure a firm balance, then licked the paw and rubbed it over his face. He would repeat the operation a dozen times or more until he was satisfied that his face passed muster, remaining rigidly upright all the time. He was now not only able to do what a normal cat cannot achieve – sit bolt upright on his hams – but he could maintain this unique position for minutes on end, looking this way or that as anything might catch his eye, the more than half-useless front flipper draped diagonally across his chest.

A cat normally stretches its limbs after a sleep by digging the claws of its front paws into the ground, carpet (or even the back of an upholstered chair until it has been cured of this destructive habit) and then pulling backwards against them. Having no viable front paws, Uncle Whiskers could no longer do this. Instead he regularly stretched himself upwards, upwards, upwards, whilst sitting on his haunches, until he looked almost incredibly tall and attenuated.

Uncle Whiskers strongly resented using an earth-box to meet the demands of nature. For some weeks after his accident he had no choice but once he recovered some mobility he would always plod off to the kitchen door and start mewing softly to be let out. During daylight we used to allow him to go unless the weather was very wet, watching over him whilst he limped off to a border and dug himself some sort of a hole. With his sole, half-paralysed front leg he found this hole-digging business very difficult at first, although he became more proficient as time went by. He would sit half-upright on his haunches and flip away with the front leg with great vigour and at least some success. Then he would rest that leg and one could see the stump of his missing leg working away under the fur, all to no purpose, of course. Uncle Whiskers, as I believe this story will show, was a remarkably intelligent, practical and courageous animal but all through his long life he never seemed to comprehend that all the hard work with this sewn-in stump was simply a waste of effort.

After darkness had fallen we could not risk letting him go out, so we used to place him in the earth-box whenever he went to the back-door with serious business in mind. As I have said, he did not like using the earth-box but he rapidly developed a philosophical outlook. But if he had fouled the box in any way, then even if it was partially cleaned out – in fact, to all intents and purposes, made clean – he simply refused to use it again unless he was absolutely driven to do so.

One evening Uncle Whiskers had plodded purposefully to the back-door and clearly needed to relieve himself, so I picked him up and put him in his box. He settled comfortably down on the dry earth, the twisted foreleg lodged over the wooden edge of the box, and proceeded to contemplate the universe. Even Uncle Whiskers, like all the rest of us, could be contrary at times. However, whilst I was waiting somewhat impatiently for the cat to get on with the job an idea flashed into my mind. I fetched an old saucer from the kitchen and then made encouraging noises of the 'come on, good boy, come on' variety, being anxious to get back to my fireside chair and a book.

Rather to my surprise, Uncle Whiskers responded to my plea for some action, proceeding to dig vigorously with his forepaw (and the stump of the other working overtime as well) until he was satisfied with his preparation and squatted down. I immediately inserted the saucer underneath him, whereupon he half-rose and gazed at me in a somewhat aggrieved kind of way. However, he resettled himself almost immediately and proceeded to relieve himself in the saucer. When he lifted himself off at the conclusion of the operation it was a simple task to empty the contents into the water-closet, rinse the saucer clean and leave it handy beside the earth-box ready for the next occasion.

In this way the earth-box was never again soiled unless Uncle Whiskers was shut in alone for a very long period or else was 'taken short' in the middle of the night. This latter contingency seldom arose, for he was a creature of exceptionally regular habits. He only required to pass water twice daily, early in the morning and again late in the afternoon and he usually combined the major operation of the day with one or the other of these outings. As he always had a deep-rooted objection to attending to these private matters indoors he could usually contain himself for several hours should he find himself shut up in the house for a long period, which was not very often. In his toilet arrangements he was about the least troublesome cat I have ever known and I rather fancy he might well be unique in being prepared to use the equivalent of a chamber-pot, indoors, from this time on until his death eleven years later. And unlike the majority of very small bairns, he learnt to use the 'potty' at the first attempt.

Uncle Whiskers, like all cats, was fastidious about these private operations. After they were concluded he spent some time covering them up with earth. Most cats with a proper set of forepaws can do this quickly but Uncle Whiskers, with only the one very gammy forepaw, took a lot longer.

Until the introduction of the saucer he always went through this covering-up routine not only outside but when he was compelled to use the earth-box. With the saucer, however, the earth was left as clean and as fresh as ever. Although he might take a sniff or two, just to make sure, he never wasted any time in trying to cover up something which he was obviously aware was not there, although when outside he followed the usual routine. He was thus already intelligent enough to overcome a deep-rooted natural instinct whenever it served no purpose.

Uncle Whiskers spent a good deal of his time in the house during that first winter following his accident – certainly much more than he would have liked. Although he could now plod about the house, jump up on chairs, beds and window-sills and even perform a fair imitation of a sprint when going upstairs, his degree of mobility was still only fractional compared with that of a normal cat. He had, however, made great progress from the virtually immobile state in which he had been returned to us by the vet at the end of September. He was certainly now capable of thoroughly enjoying himself in a restricted sort of way, giving every evidence of being happy enough in spite of manifest handicaps, always breaking into a purr of delight even if he was only spoken to, let alone fondled. At least my first, very real, fears that he might have been condemned to lead a life of misery had by now been proved absolutely groundless. His biggest difficulty lay in getting down from any height. If, for instance, he jumped off a chair his maimed foreleg was useless as a means of taking any weight or buffering the shock. He used to land on his chest with a horrible thud, followed by a quite frightening snoring grunt as the breath was involuntarily expelled from his lungs. However, the performance, horrifying though it was to watch, did not appear to hurt him, for as soon as he had landed he would set off in the direction he had made up his mind to go, 'rowing' away with his gammy forepaw. Only in moments of over-enthusiasm did he try to move his very strong hind legs too fast so that, as he had done so frequently only a few months earlier, he turned a somersault. Even this no longer seemed to upset him. It was fortunate that, even over a long period when he was unable to take any exercise, he never put on an ounce of superfluous weight. He remained a lightweight throughout his life.

As the winter gave way to spring and the days grew both longer and warmer it became more and more obvious that Uncle Whiskers was frustrated by his somewhat restricted life and was becoming desperately anxious to get out and about, as he had always been able to do for the first year of his life. Whilst we breakfasted he would sit up on his haunches for minutes on end, peering out through the french windows, watching the birds and anything else which might be moving about in the garden. As I have explained, at this time we had only dared to allow him to wander abroad when either my wife or I could spare the time to keep a constant eye on his exploits. At week-ends I gave a pretty good whack of my time to this somewhat monotonous but rewarding job. In cold weather, nevertheless, merely standing about for much of the time could be unpleasant because, unlike the cat, one did not enjoy the advantage of a first-class fur coat. My wife did her stints when I was away during the working week and I have no doubt that these frequent outdoor forays were not only much enjoyed by Uncle Whiskers but that they helped greatly in strengthening his muscles and in enabling him the better to co-ordinate the movements of his good hind legs and the one apology for a foreleg which still remained to him. What a vital possession of his was that wonky front-limb! It may have been half-paralysed, twisted and, even at its best, more than half-useless, yet almost everything depended upon it so far as Uncle Whiskers' future was concerned. My own philosophy is never to worry about disasters that may never happen but throughout the whole twelve years of his life after the disastrous accident I must admit that I was haunted by fears that that one remnant of a foreleg might get crushed or broken in some way or another or else that it might wither away completely through lack of proper use.

There we were then, in the spring of 1961 and it seemed imperative to try to give Uncle Whiskers a chance to spend much more time out-of-doors, with at least some prospect, however restricted, of prowling round a bit and getting plenty of exercise. Fortunately I had a roll of wire, about fifteen yards long, lying idle in our garden-shed and of a mesh certainly small enough to ensure that the cat, for all his ingenuity and persistence, would be unable to force his way through it. So I cut about fifteen useful stakes, pointed them and then drove them into the ground, about a yard apart, in the shape of a rough circle. I then stapled the wire-netting to the stakes, thus making a small but pleasant enclosure in the rough grasses of the orchard in which Uncle Whiskers would be able to enjoy any sunshine that was going, seek a bit of shade if it got too hot and have at least a chance of prowling around and watching what was going on in between cat-naps. My last job was to peg down the wire securely all round the base of the enclosure, so that Uncle Whiskers could not possibly force his way underneath it and then fashion some rough-and-ready but effective clips to fasten the gap after he had been placed in the pen.

One Saturday morning early in March this new paddock, admittedly without any official ceremony, was formally opened when Uncle Whiskers was deposited in it for the first time. Rough-and-ready as the workmanship was, I was pleased with my handiwork and although we still intended to allow the cat to range freely about the garden whenever we could spare the time to supervise his activities, it was gratifying to feel that he could now enjoy at least some sense of freedom at any hour of the day.

Uncle Whiskers seemed pleased, too. He stood up on his haunches, surveying the world around him through the wire. As the top of the wire was fully three feet above ground and as the cat could not possibly get over, under or through it, it was perfectly safe to leave him to enjoy his own devices. After all, when the summer came and the weather warmed up there might well be a few shrews rustling furtively about in the long grasses and doubtless they would entertain him greatly even if he no longer possessed the equipment to catch them.

All went uncommonly well for several weeks. Uncle Whiskers obviously enjoyed his long hours in the pen, prowling about and only occasionally showing signs of frustration because of its restrictions, biffing and even biting at the restraining wire-netting, occasionally even trying to dig a tunnel underneath it with a forepaw which was wholly inadequate for the purpose. On warm days he often slept for much of the time, wearied by much activity whilst awake. But he became more active as the time for his evening meal drew near and he had usually had enough of the great outdoors when we brought him in for the night.

Then, one Saturday morning, I put Uncle Whiskers in his enclosure and went indoors to my study to get on with some urgent work which I had in hand at the time. My wife had gone shopping in town and I got so deeply engrossed in my task that I lost all sense of time. It was two hours later when I remembered the cat and went downstairs and into the garden for a routine check. Before she had left my wife had placed a saucer of milk in the pen in case the cat got thirsty in the warm sunshine. Apart from that saucer the enclosure was empty. It was clear that, somehow or other, Uncle Whiskers had made his escape. He might, at this very moment, be out in the road and in grave danger of being run over. He might even have been run over already. In a perspiring palsy of fear I rushed out into the lane, calling him by name. He was nowhere to be seen. I climbed up the steep bank opposite and peered out over the big meadow beyond but there was nothing visible except the shimmering heat-haze dancing under the heat of the midday sun. In what might be fairly described as a bit of a tizzy I began to search systematically through the orchard and garden. Finally I went all round the house in case he had chosen to come indoors. Uncle Whiskers had vanished.

One of the worst human failings is that most of us tend to take things for granted. It was only now that he was missing that I really appreciated that Uncle Whiskers had come to mean very much more to me than ever any other domestic pet had done or, for that matter, is ever likely to do. He had, after all, been so near to death, followed by weeks of immobility during which he had – and there is no anthropomorphism in this – shown not only remarkable resilience, intelligence and will-power but also a good deal of courage and fortitude. True, we had spent many hours in trying to assist and encourage him to overcome his crippling injuries but it was the resolute persistence of Uncle Whiskers himself to try to do things and to stumble and tumble along, however slowly and painfully, to reach places where he wanted to be which had really been the cornerstone of his progress. Perhaps now he had indeed got somewhere to which he wished to go but, although I hunted high and low, I could not find out where it was. I cursed myself for my laxity in not keeping a sharper eye on him.

I went on with my seeking, going over ground already covered, again and again. Then, suddenly, I thought of the summerhouse. At the back of this there was an old sideboard left behind by an earlier tenant and now littered on its top with all sorts of odds and ends, from trowels and hand-forks to lubricating oil and a big roll of binder-twine. Comfortably seated on the top of the binder-twine was Uncle Whiskers, purring happily, and evincing considerable evidence of his interest in the commotion that had been going on around him. I took him up, crooking my left arm, laying him along it with his head resting on my left shoulder, and marched him back to his enclosure. He sang all the way, as if he were as pleased as punch with his escapade. When I deposited him in the pen he proceeded to lap up his milk as if nothing untoward had happened. I checked up that the wire was intact and, feeling much relieved, left him to it and went indoors to prepare our lunch.

Over the meal, the escape was the main topic for discussion. As Uncle Whiskers could not possibly have got *over* the wire, how had he gained his freedom? I had checked on all the wire-pegs which held the netting down and was sure that he had not pushed his way underneath it. However, that he *had* got out was a fact, so after we had finished our meal and washed-up we both went into the garden with the intention of carrying out a careful check of every bit of the wiring in order to satisfy ourselves that there was not some small opening through which the cat might have squeezed his way to liberty.

It was a sound idea – except for the fact that the enclosure was once again without a tenant and there was no sign of Uncle Whiskers in the vicinity of it. So another hunt started, although this time there were two hounds instead of one. Together we combed the whole of the garden, the lane, the meadow beyond, as well as the gardens of our neighbours, some of whom joined in the proceedings. I looked, full of hope, into the summerhouse to see if Uncle Whiskers had settled down again on the roll of binder-twine but he had not. A hunt of this kind may have its initial momentum and fire, after which it tends to slow down because so many likely places have already been drawn blank but it does not easily come to an end. About the most constructive remark that began to pass between my wife and myself was: 'Where *can* he be?' At last, although with reluctance, we reached the conclusion that there was nothing more to be done; we could only hope that, in his own time, Uncle Whiskers would make a safe return. He surely could not have wandered far in his crippled state and had probably settled to sleep in some sunny corner that we could not find. He had always had a pretty good 'bump' for locality and would not get lost. So long as we kept an eye on the road, where he might so easily get run down again, about the only danger seemed to lie in his being 'worried' by some aggressive cur-dog.

Although we did not admit it to one another, we were both still anxious and our uneasiness grew as the afternoon dragged on. At last, unable to settle any longer, we waddled around in an aimless kind of way, prodding with sticks into cover that was not thick enough to hide a weasel, let alone a full-grown cat. But in the end the exercise paid off. For the umpteenth time I went back to the summerhouse and searched around all the old junk that we had accumulated over the years. Quite by chance just as I was leaving, I glanced upwards towards the roof and there, stretched out in luxuriant ease on a shelf not more than six inches wide, was Uncle Whiskers, wide-eyed and purring with delight. That shelf was fully seven feet above floor-level and he could only have reached it by jumping on the sideboard, the top of which was a good three feet high, and then achieving a four-foot spring to land safely on the narrow shelf.

If he could perform a four-foot jump it seemed just possible that Uncle Whiskers could leap over the wire round his enclosure. Yet we were not at all sure that that was the manner in which he had made his escape, in spite of all this remarkable evidence of his growing strength. Jumping three or four feet from a firm base on to an equally firm footing was one thing. Jumping from rough grass, clearing a three foot hurdle and then dropping three foot on the other side, without any means of breaking the shock of the fall, seemed to both of us to be quite another. Time would tell, but, in the meanwhile, we returned him to the pen and, purring happily, he settled himself down until the evening, when we let him enjoy his supervised 'constitutional' and then brought him in for dinner.

The following morning, which was as pleasant and sunny as its predecessor, we put Uncle Whiskers in the enclosure. Then I took the Sunday newspaper and a deck-chair to a quiet part of the orchard from which I could watch Uncle Whiskers in any part of his pen. I had hardly settled before it was obvious that the cat was in a restless mood. He wandered round the inside perimeter of the netting, often sitting up on his haunches and peering into the outside world. Once or twice he attempted, with great vigour and persistence, to push his way beneath the wire but my pegging-down thwarted this move. After a few minutes he moved to a spot about three feet inside the wire, then sat up on his haunches, for all the world as if he were weighing up the chances of his next move. Quite suddenly he crouched down, then sprang off his hind legs in a flying leap, clearing the top of the wire by the best part of a foot and landing, with a thump, at least a yard beyond the netting. Although I was probably sitting eight or nine yards away, I could clearly hear the loud grunt as the air was expelled from his lungs as he landed on his chest. If the sound of the fall hurt me it certainly did not hurt Uncle Whiskers. He knew exactly where he intended to go, setting off for the summer-house, 'rowing' himself determinedly forward on his one gammy foreleg. Within two or three minutes he had ensconced himself on the high shelf on which we had found

49

him on the previous afternoon. I had crept up and watched him take the two big jumps in his stride – first up on to the top of the sideboard; then, almost without a pause, the bigger leap on to the high shelf. Although the shelf was only six inches wide, he had no difficulty in turning himself round so that he could sit in a position that gave him a better view of the outside world. When he caught sight of me he burst into a roaring purr. I could only congratulate him on a remarkable performance. The two leaps from the summerhouse floor to the shelf were not as astonishing as his escape from the pen, when he had not only easily cleared a three foot hurdle but had covered fully six feet from take-off to touch-down. Later on he was going to do even better, but sufficient unto the day! I was jubilant. It was less than nine months since the accident. All those winter games with the ping-pong ball up and down the stairs had certainly paid off.

As it was now obvious that Uncle Whiskers could escape from the wired enclosure at will, there was clearly a problem to be solved without delay. With a little ingenuity and some hard work it would obviously have been possible to wire over the top of the enclosure, thus making it impossible for the cat to jump out of it. But the pen only occupied a few paltry square yards and it seemed clear to me that Uncle Whiskers' strength had outgrown it. Whilst one had to think of his safety, it was unthinkable to imprison a young and healthy cat, not yet two years old, perhaps until he died. All our neighbours were friendly enough. The only major risk in giving Uncle Whiskers his liberty, at any rate by day, lay in the proximity of the road. We finally agreed that we must allow him his freedom, at the same time doing our best to convince him that the dangerous road was 'out of bounds'. So I rolled up the wire, collected the stakes and pegs and that was the end of the enclosure in which Uncle Whiskers had enjoyed quite a lot of fun over two or three months. Perhaps even more important was the fact that he had been given the opportunity to develop his powerful hind legs and make progress in his locomotion, which still rested on better co-ordination between his powerful hindquarters and that one weak, twisted, half-paralysed foreleg.

It was at about this time that Uncle Whiskers really began to develop into a feline philosopher. If he wandered towards the road, one of us would fetch him back and put him in the back-garden, where he seemed quite content, even if he had had his mind changed for him, to take up some other ploy, such as hunting shrews in the rougher grasses of the orchard or trying to pounce on grasshoppers or cabbage-white butterflies. Probably because he was now able to get all the exercise he wanted during the long days of summer he was developing his powers with astonishing speed. Above the elbow of his one withered foreleg he started to gain considerable muscular power and could even row himself along, over short distances, as fast as or faster than a walking-pace. His huge hams had developed into power houses of muscle, so that he had no difficulty at all in leaping up three or four feet. It was astonishing, too, to watch him jump down the four feet from his favourite shelf in the summerhouse on to the old sideboard. Then, after sitting for a minute or two bolt upright on his haunches, surveying the prospect and perhaps using the opportunity to wash his face, he would jump down the three feet on to the hard, concrete floor.

I have heard it said that even an ordinary cat, when jumping down from a fair height on to a hard surface, can seriously injure the lower jawbone. This may be so but Uncle Whiskers, with no forepaws to land on, performed this feat regularly for almost twelve years and never came to any harm but, as I hope is clear already, he was a very intelligent fellow. However, possessing a high degree of intelligence is one thing; the ability to exploit it to the full is quite another. Uncle Whiskers had achieved some very remarkable performances since, miraculously, he had returned almost from the dead the previous September. Watching him galumphing about the garden, leaping a yard into the air and covering two, in – admittedly unsuccessful – attempts to land on a shrew or some other quarry made it almost difficult to believe that, when he had been returned by the vet, he had been unable even to move off the hearthrug. There was relatively little that we had been able to do to assist his rehabilitation. He had had to teach himself, to learn the hard way, by experience. It was often a hard way indeed but Uncle Whiskers was tough as well as intelligent. I doubt if we had even an inkling of it at that time, but Uncle Whiskers was on the threshold of a life of high adventure. He was shortly to show us that an intelligent cat with two good hind legs and nothing 'up front' except for a single, twisted, nerveless limb could perform much better than can the average cat with all four limbs sound.

I have related that, since his accident, we had never dared to let Uncle Whiskers out at night. However, as we approached that midsummer of 1961, the light mornings and the long evenings were a great temptation for him, especially the latter. I have, myself, always preferred to be in bed and asleep long before midnight and I like to be up and about around six o'clock or very soon after. In high summer, however, daylight arrives between four and five o'clock and Uncle Whiskers duly noted this fact. At night, instead of sleeping on the end of the bed, he now slept on the top, curled up into the small of my back. Like me, he was a good sleeper, seldom stirring after he had purred himself to sleep, but if and when he did move he usually woke me up.

In the dark days of winter I was usually on the move

long before Uncle Whiskers, but once the early dawns arrived he took it into his head that it was high time to be up and about. I nipped this idea in the bud. When he stirred, and awoke me in doing so, he would sit up on his haunches, giving relief to his sleep-stiffened limbs with one of his gigantic stretches, slowly raising himself upwards until his body became so thin and attenuated that it almost looked as if it must snap. I would watch him with a wary eye. The moment he contracted himself, sinking slowly back to something like normal, he would usually make a move to jump down from the bed. I would say, very sharply, 'No!' Uncle Whiskers had long ago learnt that this meant, roughly speaking, 'Stop what you intend to do, because it will get you nowhere', for when, in earlier days, he had disobeyed the injunction, I had *always* put him back where he had started. So when I said 'No' in the pearly light of a summer's dawn he would suddenly check his departure off the bed, turn towards me and eye me quizzically, as if he were weighing up the chances of whether or not I really meant what I said. Occasionally he made a move to try his luck but if I repeated the command he would give up, cuddle himself down again to sleep and, at the same time, break out into a roaring purr, as if one had done him a favour.

If I remember rightly, we had rather few still, warm evenings in that summer of 1961. However, when we did enjoy them Uncle Whiskers went almost barmy with enthusiasm in chasing the many moths that fluttered around in the twilight. It would have been a shame to have brought him in too early, just when the main fun of his day was about to start, so I used to go out to join him around sunset. I would open a deck-chair and set it up in the entrance to the summerhouse, smoking a crepuscular pipe and being highly entertained by the cat's antics on the lawn. He was all eyes for the fluttering moths. Whenever one came even reasonably low over him he would leap up, trying vainly to strike it down with his paralysed front paw (and working away with the stump of the other one, too) and then fall back on the grass with a sickeningly heavy thud and a grunt. Those falls still hurt me when I watched them but they never seemed to bother Uncle Whiskers. He was off again at once, stumping around, ever ready to spring up into the air again on the slightest lepidopteral provocation.

Spring and miss. Spring and miss. Poor old Uncle Whiskers – he always missed! Moth or mouse, butterfly or grasshopper, he always would miss because he simply could not realize that he no longer possessed any striking paws nor any claws with which to seize the prey. I knew that he was fairly intelligent but when I used to watch him hunting those moths, so hard but so fruitlessly, I realized that instinct was more powerful than intellect. Perhaps it did not matter, because the cat was obviously having a lot of fun and healthy exercise; in a somewhat restricted way, maybe, he was still a mobile, elastic and agile creature, clearly enjoying life to the very limit of his ability. There were times when I wished that he could, by some lucky fluke, somehow capture just one moth but, as I puffed away at my pipe in the gloaming, it was satisfying enough to see him so fit and active, especially whenever I cared to recall the fact that, only nine months earlier, he couldn't move at all.

There were some warm twilights when moths were in especially good supply. Then Uncle Whiskers leapt and pranced about in pursuit of them until he was gasping for breath. He would take a brief rest, sitting up on his haunches and gazing round at me or anything else which took his fancy. On these occasions he had his tail stretched straight out behind him and he now had no difficulty in maintaining this most unfeline but highly engaging posture, without ever losing his balance, for as long as he chose to do so.

He was also able to turn his head until he was looking directly behind – an extraordinary position in which he took on an almost owl-like appearance and one which he achieved partly by turning his head on his neck and partly by twisting his body from the hips. He would soon recover his breath from previous exertions and if a moth came fluttering along he would contract his body, still squatting on his haunches, waiting until it was almost overhead before he unwound himself in a flying leap. He missed again, for sure. Yet one day, surely, his useless, flipping forepaw would, by a stroke of luck, hit a moth and knock it down. It never happened that way. But Uncle Whiskers did learn to catch moths, and this was the way of it.

It was one of those still, clear summer evenings, cool enough after the heat of the day to feel almost crisp. Moths were not in good supply. I had watched Uncle Whiskers, not best-pleased with the moth famine, leaping up at two or three of them as they passed him by. Then, quite unexpectedly (for both of us, I think) Uncle Whiskers leapt up and snapped at and succeeded in catching a fair-sized moth in his mouth. He fell with it, thudding on to the hard turf with his chest, the force of the fall expelling all the wind from his lungs which, in turn, blew the moth out of his mouth. The moth was injured and fluttered rather purposelessly over the short grass but even before the idea had entered my head to give it the benefit of a mercy-killing, Uncle Whiskers had taken a gigantic leap and, with astonishingly good judgement of the jump, landed so precisely that he was able to seize the insect in his mouth. He must have given it a killing crunch and disliked the taste. He spat it out and the dead moth lay in front of him. After hundreds, if not thousands of vain leapings, that one dead moth meant a great deal to Uncle Whiskers. He wriggled and rolled about in a great ecstasy of triumph and when I called him a 'fine boy-o' he rolled about even more and burst into a great purr of happiness. Intelligence overcame instinct, so far as Uncle Whiskers was concerned. As far as I know he never again attempted to catch and kill by trying to use striking paws that he had lost forever when only just over a year old. It was the teeth that could do the trick – and now he knew it. So far as his hunting was concerned, Uncle Whiskers had suddenly changed from a cat to a terrier.

Whether one likes it or not, one has to go where one's work takes one. At the end of that summer of 1961 my wife and I had to move to a large house, surrounded by pleasant grounds, in the Midlands. On our last night in our old home there was no moth-hunting. Instead we had a first-class electrical storm. Uncle Whiskers always hated thunder. The next day we set off northwards. Uncle Whiskers, of course, went with us.

V

Apart from the journey to the vet after his accident (when he had been almost unconscious from shock and pain) and the three miles back again a week later, Uncle Whiskers had never been on any travels. During the long journey by road he was at pains to show us that he hated it. He lay in his wicker basket quietly enough until we started to move. From then on he never ceased protesting for more than a minute or two, whether he was in the basket, let out to prowl around the baggage on the rear seats or stroked on a knee. If I could have foreseen the fuss he was going to kick up I should have got the vet to provide some tranquillizing pills. I think the unlucky cat, because of his injuries, may have experienced acute difficulty in balancing himself against the swaying and lurchings of the car. Anyway, he loathed it all and was obviously uncomfortable although, mercifully, not sick.

The big house to which we went with our few sticks of furniture was being changed into offices. It was not to be our permanent home but we were occupying two or three singularly inconvenient rooms whilst we hunted for a place of our own . . . a task that took us over a year. On our arrival, whilst waiting for the furniture-van to catch up with us, we put Uncle Whiskers into what was to be, temporarily, our tiny spare bedroom and presented him with a saucerful of creamy milk and a plateful of scalded liver. However much he had been upset by the journey Uncle Whiskers recovered his poise immediately, demolishing the liver as if he hadn't eaten for a week and then scoffing the milk at one go. We put a cushion on the bare floor and shut him in. A few minutes later, to our relief, he was curled up and fast asleep.

By teatime we had more or less dug ourselves in and after the commotion was over we let Uncle Whiskers out into his new world. He was now capable of rowing himself along at a steady pace for long periods and the distances that he could cover, even if rather slowly, surprised us. The house was set in many acres of ground and how Uncle Whiskers loved those quiet, open spaces, the great areas of rough grasses, bracken and heather, not to mention the sunny lawns and the herbaceous borders on the south side. Hazards from road-traffic were minimal. The only public road was half a mile distant and the amount of traffic on the drive up to the house was small and almost entirely confined to the working day.

There was, however, one feature which caused us considerable anxiety at first. Sunk in the spacious lawns on the south side of the house was a large pool, once a swimming-pool, which was many feet deep at one end. If Uncle Whiskers was to fall into this pool then, unless human aid was handy, his chance of getting out alive was absolutely nil. It would have been criminal, however, to imprison this adventurous cat indoors except on the few occasions when an eye could be kept on him, apart from the fact that human company completely spoils the sport for any hunting cat. So we let him take his chances, of which tumbling into the pool was one.

It so happened that my own office overlooked the lawns and the old swimming-pool. Being an early riser, I sometimes took the opportunity of doing an hour's work before breakfast. On one of these mornings, not long after our arrival, I chanced to look out of my window just as Uncle Whiskers was returning from a naturally unsuccessful but no doubt enjoyable early morning foray among the rabbits which, in spite of suffering from that abominable, man-inflicted scourge of myxomatosis, were plentiful and did much damage to the lawns and flower-beds.

I watched Uncle Whiskers plod across the dew-covered grass until he arrived at one end of the long pool. All round the pool there was a stone parapet, about a foot in width so far as I recall it. These stones edging the pool divided the lawns from the sheer drop into the deep waters. Uncle Whiskers must have learnt very quickly that, whenever the grass was wet with dew or rain, it was much pleasanter to break a part of the journey by travelling along the stonework. This was, however, the first occasion when I had watched him and I admit that I was horribly uneasy.

Arriving on the narrow stonework, Uncle Whiskers proceeded to sit up on his haunches and survey the scene. Then still sitting upright, he proceeded to wash his underparts which were doubtless saturated by his travels over the wet grass. I couldn't help wondering what might happen should he be suddenly frightened by the appearance of some cur-dog or even a fox. Might he not tumble to his doom into the water? Might he not do ditto if he simply missed his footing? By and by when he had finished his washing, he started to plod back to his breakfast, keeping to the dry stonework along the water's edge, occasionally pausing to peer into the mysterious and somewhat murky depths or standing high on his haunches to survey the outlook. He was happy enough and seemed brimful of confidence, so what useful purpose could possibly be served by worrying on his behalf – worrying which, if allowed to run riot, might only result in the curtailment of the very liberty from which he got so much of his fun. Fate had, after all, already limited his freedom to a considerable extent and to interfere further in that direction would surely be inexcusable. Neither man nor any animal can enjoy life to the full without taking some risks to life or limb.

Uncle Whiskers now had enormous scope for his activities and this gave him the opportunity to overcome his severe physical handicaps to such a degree that he was soon to become more successful as a hunter than the majority of his kind. Perhaps it may still be difficult for the reader fully to comprehend how a cat without any effective forelegs could possibly overcome such a grievous handicap but Uncle Whiskers certainly did so. We had arrived at our new residence when the late summer days were still long and the cat usually wanted to go out as soon as dawn broke. He would be absent for an hour or so, exploring his new and intriguing domains, returning at breakfast time with the appetite of a tiger. He would spend a good part of the day sleeping, indoors if it were wet and outside, tucked away in one of the many retreats known only to himself, if the sun shone. In the late afternoon, when all was quiet again, he would go off on the prowl, usually returning for his supper about sunset or soon after. By that time he was fairly weary from his long travels and was happy enough to stay indoors and sleep until daybreak; it was only when the days really started to shorten that he became something of a night-bird.

During the first week or two we did not believe that he travelled very far. However, his rapidly increasing energies and adventurousness during that summer of 1961 had one unfortunate result. Because the only front limb remaining to him was paralysed from the elbow down, the uncontrollable foot turned in on itself. Instead of rowing himself forward on the pads of this leg, therefore, the main friction fell on the back of the 'wrist'. Here the fur had been worn away completely and the skin had opened into a sore. The more active he was, the more inflamed and ugly this became. It was a cause for real anxiety, because if anything should happen to his one remaining, decrepit foreleg it seemed that even the indomitable Uncle Whiskers would be rendered immobile and as it was hard to believe that any cat could have anything but a miserable existence under such circumstances, it would probably have been necessary, in all kindness, to have had him put down. Having travelled with him so far, so to speak, from the very edge of a youthful death, the blackest thought of all was the idea of having to have him destroyed, however humanely. The preservation of that front foreleg was vital to the preservation of Uncle Whiskers himself.

My wife sewed up a number of short, linen socklets. Whenever Uncle Whiskers went out one of these was tied, by means of a tape 'built-in' to the top of the sock, on to his gammy leg. It would have been more effective and probably easier to have used elastic instead of tape, but we were frightened of impeding the circulation in a limb which was wonky enough already. Uncle Whiskers, usually one of the most philosophical and tractable of creatures, took great exception to wearing these socklets. Although he was much too well-mannered to raise objections whilst being togged up for an outing, as soon as he was outside the house he would sit up on his haunches and wrestle away at the sock with his sharp teeth. In the long run he often succeeded in loosening the tape and getting rid of what he seemed to regard as a stupid and ignominious encumbrance, although it mostly remained on long enough to assist in the slow healing of the sore on the foot. We reckoned that he lost a sock on about half of his forays. Some of these were subsequently recovered and could be used again but replacements had to be tailored at the rate of about half a dozen a week.

The recovery of some of these white socks gave us welcome proof that, even during his first weeks in this new home, Uncle Whiskers was really in remarkably good fettle. It was a common-place to find a sock three or four hundred yards from the house and, apart from the fact that the cat probably got rid of many of them quite early on in an excursion, he seldom travelled in anything resembling a straight line, making various and often long diversions in order to investigate this interesting matter or that one. He certainly had plenty of things to fascinate him. Although myxomatosis took a big toll, there were many rabbits around the house, in all sizes from youngsters to big bucks. Uncle Whiskers was much taken up with them when, mostly at dawn and dusk, they emerged from cover to feed on the lawns and to work their mischief in the flower borders. He would squat among them, wide-eyed and alert, and the rabbits seemed to regard him as quite harmless and innocuous – and so he was, rabbit-wise, in those early days. Circumstances changed very soon, but I must not anticipate.

Keen as he was as a hunter and although he had now learnt that the only way in which he could seize and kill his prey was by using his teeth, for some weeks Uncle Whiskers caught nothing more remarkable than a few butterflies and moths and the odd mouse and shrew. Lepidoptera were merely practice targets. He objected to having them in his mouth and only his urge to hunt overcame this distaste. He never ate either a mouse or a shrew but brought them back over long distances to deposit them on the doorstep. He would then sit upright on his haunches and flip the door with his forepaw so violently that he could raise quite a noise. If, by any chance, this brought no response, he would leap up on to the ledge of our sitting-room window and bang away at it in fine style. The moment he saw anybody move he would jump down so that, by the time one of us had got to the door and opened it, he would be standing upright over his dead quarry, immensely proud of himself and fairly singing his head off with delight. The moment he was congratulated he would roll about on the ground in sheer ecstasy, raising no objection when you seized the prey by its tail and took it off to the kitchen fire for cremation.

One week-end afternoon in September we were sitting over tea when I heard Uncle Whiskers rapping on the door with his flipper. I went to open it, wondering if I should have the pleasure of congratulating him on catching a mouse or shrew which he would have deposited, as usual, on the doorstep. There was nothing on the step but when I opened the door wide to welcome Uncle Whiskers in to the home, he immediately turned away, moving towards a small courtyard at the western end of the house. I watched him, puzzled by his behaviour. After he had rowed himself rapidly and with obvious intent for a few paces he looked round at me, then sat up on his haunches, gazing first directly at me, then towards the courtyard which was hidden from me by the corner of the house. Then he gazed back at me again. As I still did not move, he stumped two or three paces back towards me, then repeated the sitting-up performance.

I was intrigued by this curious behaviour, so I walked out. The moment I moved in his direction, Uncle Whiskers set off towards the courtyard at his very best pace, which was now equal, over short distances, to a brisk walk. He led me round the angle of the house and diagonally across the yard. Even before he reached it I spotted the body of the dead rat. He went on up to it, then sat up and stood over it, gammy forepaw dangling across his chest, looking from the rat to me and then back again as much as to say: 'All my own work, you know!' When I congratulated him in my most dulcet, 'good boy' tone of voice, Uncle Whiskers went berserk. He leaped in the air and then proceeded to wriggle and roll over on his back, jerking convulsively from one side to the other, in a rare display of satisfied abandonment, the whole gymnastic exhibition being accompanied by loud, rattling purrs of delight.

'All my own work, you know!' Well, Uncle Whiskers seemed mighty pleased with himself but I didn't believe that he had killed that rat. How could he do it, when he possessed no striking paws or claws? If he had killed that rat, then the rat must have been blind and walked straight into his mouth. I don't like rats but I picked up that corpse and it was still warmish, so that it could not have been dead for more than a very few minutes. There were wounds in the neck, where a little trickle of blood had coagulated, which had surely been made by teeth. I knew that Uncle Whiskers certainly had two useful assets – fine, sharp teeth and tremendous strength in his jaws. By his behaviour (he was still rolling about at my feet like some intoxicated drunkard) he certainly gave me the impression that he had killed the rat and the deep incisions round the beast's neck could be accepted as supporting evidence. But unless the rat had literally committed suicide by running into the jaws of the cat, it was impossible to conceive how the cat could possibly have murdered it. Although Uncle Whiskers' mobility was increasing from month to month, he could not possibly have any chance of outrunning a healthy rat – nor ever would, for that matter. But I gave him the benefit of my serious doubts, tickling his tummy and singing his praises and he nearly blew his top with the excitement of it all.

A few days later there was a repeat performance. This time, however, when there was no offering on the doorstep and Uncle Whiskers stumped off towards the courtyard I had learned the drill and followed at once. He had something he wanted to show me. He led me to what he wanted me to suppose was his second rat, which displayed exactly the same symptoms in death as the first one. I found it more difficult, this time, to believe that the dead rat was not all his own work but I was still completely baffled by the problem of how he could conceivably catch and kill one with his limited armament and mobility. I presumed that he did not bring the rats back to the doorstep, as he always had done with mice and shrews, because they were too heavy for him. I was wrong. Uncle Whiskers loathed rats and once he had caught and killed one he would hurl it aside and never touch it again. He seldom ate mice and shrews but when he had killed one he would often toss the corpse up into the air several times before he set off home to present it to us. But he would scarcely sniff at a rat once he had killed it, let alone carry it back to the house.

Although he still roamed far afield and spent some of his time, especially for an hour or so after daybreak, among his beloved (?) rabbits, Uncle Whiskers began to haunt that courtyard and I was lucky enough to be able to watch the way in which he stalked and killed his third rat. He was sitting, waiting and watching, somewhere near the middle of the courtyard. The irregular configuration of the house blocked the east side of the courtyard and around the southern and western sides there was a high brick wall at the end of which were a pair of wrought-iron gates giving access to the greenhouses and a walled garden.

Whilst I was watching, standing stock-still at the angle of the house, a fat rat slipped under the gate and started to move down close under the base of the west wall. Although he scarcely twitched a muscle, I got the strong impression that Uncle Whiskers was aware of the entry of the rat almost at once. I think he may have moved his head very slightly, in order to get the rat squarely in his sights. Certainly he followed the unsuspecting rodent as it moved slowly and furtively towards the south-west corner of the courtyard, for I could see Uncle Whiskers gently, almost imperceptibly, moving his head to follow the rat's movements. Apart from this movement of the head he might have been carved out of a piece of marble, not even betraying his excitement by even the twitch of his tail-tip.

The rat went on slowly moving down under the west wall until it was three-quarters of the way to the corner where the south wall made a right-angle with it. Until then Uncle Whiskers made no real movement but now he rose up on his haunches and remained looking at his intended victim. I think the rat became aware of the cat almost at once. Certainly the rat paused, turned half-round, and appeared to be looking at Uncle Whiskers, although the two were still fully seven or eight yards apart – perhaps more. Had the rat chosen, at that moment, to bolt back under the wall and through the gate I am sure that Uncle Whiskers would not have had the remotest chance of getting to terms with it. I would make a shrewd guess that this particular feline mind had no intention of letting his instincts get the better of his hard-earned reason and was content to play a waiting game. Had he moved at this juncture, it must have been odds on that the rat would have bolted back to safety. Uncle Whiskers, still sitting up on his haunches, hardly twitched a whisker. What followed was not only both fascinating and thrilling but it proved to my satisfaction that I was the owner of a cat with an exceptionally high feline IQ.

Uncle Whiskers, after that long pause sitting up rigid

on his haunches, lowered himself very slowly to the ground. Almost imperceptibly and certainly very cautiously, with prolonged and frequent pauses, he entered upon a stalk which lasted several minutes. He moved (perhaps shuffled might be the better word) not diagonally across the court-yard directly towards the rat but towards the west wall, on a track which would lead him to a position between his quarry and the gate under which it had entered the yard. When he was two or three yards from the wall, Uncle Whiskers came to a stop, settled down and remained motionless, facing towards the rat. If the rat chose to bolt back under the wall to the gateway it crossed my mind that Uncle Whiskers might try a prodigious leap but he could not be quick enough to intercept his prey. I was a little worried that, should he try such a leap, he might well bash his brains out against the brick wall. It was a very tense, if slow-moving, drama.

Cat and rat, both scarcely twitching a whisker, stared at one another over a distance of several yards for what seemed a long time. I, myself, scarcely dared to breath. Then the rat crept very slowly a little farther along under the west wall, away from the gate and also away from the cat. With almost exaggerated caution Uncle Whiskers proceeded to close the distance, then squatted again, now within about six feet of the wall. To cut a longish story a little short, the rat again shifted, followed slowly by the cat, until eventually the former was in the corner of the angle of the west and south walls with Uncle Whiskers facing it, still two yards from the west wall but three or four from the southern one. If the rat chose to bolt under the south wall, it seemed impossible that the cat could leap at it, although he might still be able to cut off its retreat.

There was another long pause, with neither party apparently prepared to make a move. Suddenly, unexpectedly, the rat made a bolt for it under the west wall, intent on going back the way he had come and making his escape through the gate. I had been watching the rat rather than the cat but I saw Uncle Whiskers airborne in a flying leap. A split second later I thought there was a squeak and Uncle Whiskers had his teeth into the rat. The rat, however, was still very much alive. It even succeeded in dragging the cat round, for Uncle Whiskers had no forepaws to steady himself. It was a good-sized rat and I had to hope that the cat could hold on with his sharp teeth. He managed to do so. As the rat weakened he shook it, terrier-fashion, and dragged it backwards. Since his accident Uncle Whiskers had learnt to walk backwards, shuffling on his powerful hind legs. I have never known any other cat which could perform in this way.

He had the dying rat very firmly in his vice-like jaws. Victory was at hand. He stood up on his haunches, so that only the rat's tail trailed on the ground, shaking it so violently that he momentarily lost his balance but not, luckily, his grip on his victim. Actually the rat was now as good as dead. The cat sat up on his haunches again, shook the rat several times, then flung it aside. The legs of the prey were still twitching but these were only death-reflexes. Uncle Whiskers seemed to look at it for a few seconds, as if contemplating the sheer size of his prize, then turned round and began moving towards the house with the obvious intention of fetching my wife or me to inspect the evidence of his triumph. But I was already walking towards him and I was so impressed by his almost uncanny skill that I picked him up and gave him a rare good cosseting, holding him on the crook of my arm with his head on my left shoulder. He fairly roared away in my left ear, purring his head off and when I put him down he indulged himself in a whole series of victory rolls.

There was, this time, no room to doubt that 'All my own work!' attitude of the cat. Certainly a four-legged cat could not possibly have put up a better performance, either in the patience demanded by the long stalk or in the almost incredible judgement in leaping in for the kill. Once airborne on that final leap, Uncle Whiskers could not, surely, alter his trajectory in any way. I still find it difficult to understand how he did it, but that he did there was no doubt whatsoever. He was, in effect, a two-legged cat with powerful jaws, the heart of a lion and a great deal more 'up top' than most of his kind.

Shortly after the incident in which I had watched Uncle Whiskers stalk and kill this rat, my friend Stanley Porter, wild-life photographer and naturalist, was staying with us over a week-end. In the afternoon I had gone off on some ploy or other and Stanley was roaming the grounds with his camera. By a stroke of luck he arrived at the courtyard just as Uncle Whiskers went in for the kill and nailed yet another rat. This was a smallish specimen, measuring barely a foot from snout to tail-tip but I recall that Stanley was highly excited by this exhibition of the cat's skill, especially by what he regarded, I suppose rightly, as a somewhat maimed specimen of the breed. Anyway, he took a series of photographs, including several of Uncle Whiskers rolling about in great glee after the kill. I still have these pictures, and some of the drawings which embellished the original edition of this book were based on them.

Uncle Whiskers slew a fair number of rats that autumn. But, perhaps inevitably in view of the success of the hunter, the supply of rats declined or, at any rate, those that came into the courtyard were fewer and fewer in number. He could only catch a rat, obviously, if he could more or less corner it. From time to time he continued to nail the odd rat but the sport was now insufficient in quantity to satisfy the hunter. The small wave of myxomatosis had subsided and there were still plenty of conies. For an hour or two after daybreak and again when twilight was falling, as well as on nights with a full moon, it was not uncommon to be able to count twenty or thirty prowling about on the wide lawns. Only four months had passed since Uncle Whiskers had first succeeded in catching a moth in his mouth. But he was much stronger now and had polished up his techniques. He was a mighty slayer of rats. But rabbits presented him with a totally different problem to solve. He could corner rats and catch them when they bolted. He could not corner rabbits.

We often watched Uncle Whiskers sitting, still as a stone, among feeding rabbits. For all I know he might already have attempted to spring on one but, if so, I believe it must have been abortive, because once he started killing them he always lugged them back to the house for inspection and congratulations. This is why I think that, early one morning at the end of October 1961, I watched Uncle Whiskers catch and kill his very first rabbit.

1961 was the first year when Summer Time was extended until the end of October. Uncle Whiskers used to demand to be let out at first-light, which was round about half-past six on a fine morning. Our temporary quarters in the big house were singularly inconvenient because our sitting-room and two bedrooms, on the north side of the building, were separated from our tiny kitchen, on the south side, by a long, stone-flagged passage. If Uncle Whiskers was out after dark we used to leave the kitchen window partly open and we had constructed three wooden steps so that he could climb easily on to the window ledge. We used to place a chair inside. The cat used the outer steps but spurned the chair, leaping from the window-ledge down to the floor and then padding down the passage to knock either on the sitting-room door or our bedroom door, according to whether we had turned in for the night or not. Even if it was after midnight he never found any difficulty in waking me up, banging away with his flipper in tremendous style. It seemed obvious that he had no feeling in this paw, for otherwise he would surely have hurt himself in this vigorous performance. Once I had let him into the bedroom I would pad up the passage to close and secure the kitchen window and by the time I had returned Uncle Whiskers would be sitting on the carpet beside the bed, busily engaged on his late-night toilet. I was seldom asleep before he leapt up on the bed, burst into purring and then settled himself down for the night.

Let us return to what was, for Uncle Whiskers, the very intriguing subject of rabbits. On that morning of October 1961 I had let the cat out soon after half-past six. The side-door that we used opened on to the front or north side of the house. To reach the lawns on the south side where most of the rabbits fed the cat had to traverse the whole frontage, go round the east front and so on to the south lawns – a distance, as the cat went, of at least 200 yards. I pottered around in a dressing-gown for a few minutes and then went down to the kitchen to make a cup of tea before I had my bath. Looking out of the kitchen window, in the strengthening light I could just see Uncle Whiskers away beyond the swimming-pool, at the south-eastern corner of the lawns where they were edged by big rhododendrons and other shrubs. All around him a number of rabbits were busily nibbling away at the turf. Uncle Whiskers was squatting, chin resting on the heavily dewed grass, almost motionless. Now and then he would move his head to right or left, perhaps summing up the situation in his mind, but otherwise he might have been dead.

The rabbits behaved as if they were almost unaware of his presence. I turned off the kettle and settled down to watch with the aid of a pair of binoculars. I had to be as patient as the cat. Even when the rabbits danced around he remained 'frozen'. He must have been pent-up with excitement but he did not reveal that fact by even a twitch of the tail. It was not until a fair-sized but not fully grown rabbit moved closer to him, certainly within three or four yards, that I saw him flex the muscles of his powerful hind legs. It was all over in a flash. Uncle Whiskers sprang into the air – and missed the rabbit by at least a foot as it bolted off into the nearby bushes. Uncle Whiskers made no attempt to pursue the rabbit. It would have been futile, anyway. Almost as soon as he landed he became a stone again, crouching motionless. The more distant rabbits had merely paused momentarily and then got on with their breakfasts.

I was disappointed, even a trifle annoyed, that Uncle Whiskers had missed the rabbit after his great performances with rats. I could, however, appreciate and sympathize with his difficulties. When he was ratting, the quarry had to run along under a wall, so that it had to stick to a particular line in making its bid for freedom and could only try to outwit the cat by sheer speed, which it seldom, if ever, succeeded in doing. Rabbits, on the other hand, taxed the hunter to the limit . . . if not beyond, judging by what I had just seen. He could not, as with rats, skilfully shepherd a rabbit into a corner from which it would eventually have to make a bolt for it. Uncle Whiskers' intelligence was further revealed in that, from the very outset of his successful rabbiting career, he appreciated this fact and resorted to the strategy of lying completely doggo, waiting for the quarry (and fortunately rabbits are nothing like as intelligent as rats) to come to him. However, as had just been demonstrated by his abortive leap to kill, a rabbit was free to dart off in any direction at the last, vital moment. It seemed to me that Uncle Whiskers, once committed to a flying leap, was bound to land on a certain spot – the spot where the rabbit was when he started the leap but not where it would be when he landed. Surely any sane and healthy rabbit must always be able to elude him?

My conclusions were quickly proved false.

I went on watching. Soon the rabbits were all again loping around as if the cat was really lifeless instead of merely playing possum. A good specimen, bigger than the one he had missed, came slowly towards him until it was nibbling away within six feet. This time Uncle Whiskers took his time and it was not until that split-second when he was in mid-air that I really realized that he might be in with a chance. Uncle Whiskers never carried an ounce of superfluous weight. Apart from the powerhouse at the back-end he was one of the long, lean and wiry types, never turning the scales at much more than eight or nine pounds. I was fearful that, even if he had timed his leap so well that he landed on his victim it must still be able to shake him off and make good its escape.

At a distance of something like 100 yards I could not clearly follow, even through a pair of binoculars, all that happened in the next half-minute. Uncle Whiskers certainly settled his teeth into that rabbit somewhere in the area of the neck. But the rabbit moved off pretty smartly, dragging Uncle Whiskers over several yards. Uncle Whiskers hung on desperately, but the rabbit, although he stopped dragging the cat along, was by no means done for. In the scuffling I got the impression that the rabbit was trying to shift the cat by rolling over, for at one moment Uncle Whiskers' long hind legs seemed to be sticking up in the air. The rabbit tried desperately to drag the cat along again but superior weight told in the end and those sharp teeth, sunk deep and driven home by his outstandingly powerful jaws, soon began to have their effect. The rabbit's movements first became random and then, in its death agonies, spasmodic and, finally, no more than muscular reflexes. The rabbit was dead. Long live rabbits!

Uncle Whiskers did not let go of his victim until all movement ceased. He then stood up over the corpse on his hind legs, seemingly surveying a scene from which all the rabbits had vanished. I daresay he was breathless and anxious to recover from his strenuous exertions but I felt mighty proud of him. I went down the passage and out of the side-door, anxious to get out to him and congratulate him on what was, by any standards, a magnificent performance and to carry the rabbit back for him. However, by the time I had traversed the courtyard and reached the stone-flagged path which ran all along the south side of the house I could see that Uncle Whiskers was laboriously dragging the dead rabbit back over the dewy lawn. He was obviously unaware of the fact that I had been watching him from the kitchen window and I had little doubt that the grand finale, for him, would come when he laid his quarry at my feet. 'All my own work, you know!' And this time it really was some work! I decided that it might spoil things for him if I went out to offer assistance which was probably not required. Nevertheless, Uncle Whiskers had the job of lugging a corpse which was half his own weight all of 100 yards, because factors such as the swimming-pool and the position of the steps leading up from the lawns on to the stone-flagged terrace prevented him from taking anything like a straight course for home. So I decided to watch his progress from a position where I was almost wholly hidden from him, ready to render assistance if it was really required.

Uncle Whiskers certainly made slow progress. He had seized the rabbit in his mouth by one of its ears and tried to keep it on his left side, where he had no foreleg at all to get in the way, rowing himself forward strongly with the paralysed right foreleg, backed up by his muscular hind limbs. Unfortunately the backside of the rabbit repeatedly got in the way of his back legs, so that he kept on stumbling over it, making it necessary for him to rearrange the position of the quarry until he could get moving again.

Uncle Whiskers, because of these difficulties, also tended to steer an erratic course, a veering towards his left requiring constant and laborious correction. The job was not only slow and difficult, taxing his strength to the limit, but he often had to take a 'breather', squatting upright on his haunches, dropping the rabbit temporarily, and visibly panting for breath.

The constant stumblings over his victim clearly vexed him. Although the rabbit was as dead as the proverbial doornail, I got a very strong impression that Uncle Whiskers thought that it was deliberately impeding his progress, for more than once when he tumbled over it he got a good grip of its ear and then, raising himself up as high on his haunches as he was able, he shook the rabbit so violently between his teeth that he occasionally toppled over.

I watched his progress until he had crossed the lawn and arrived at the foot of the three or four steps up on to the terrace. His journey was now more than half-accomplished but, although I had not been timing it, it had probably taken him all of ten minutes. And now he was faced with the problem of getting his heavy burden up those steps!

He got the head and shoulders of the rabbit on to the first step, its hindquarters still on the grass. He then let go of it, proceeding to climb above it. With a mighty heave, after getting hold of an ear, he got the body on to the first step. This time he did not let go of it, but proceeded, by walking backwards, to lug it on to the terrace. It was a most unfeline performance, because as I have said, cats do not usually walk backwards. It was an action bred of the injuries following his accident. Uncle Whiskers could always back directly away from anything he didn't like. Anyway, the effort of tugging the corpse up the steps necessitated yet another pause for breath and I took the opportunity to go back to the kitchen to await his triumphant arrival. At this stage he had no idea that I had watched his great success.

I deliberately kept well back from the window but as he got near to it I could hear him snuffling along with his burden, occasionally gasping for breath or grumbling throatily when, probably, he once again stumbled over the rabbit. I wondered how he would negotiate the three wooden steps up to the window sill, but I didn't dare look out in case I gave the game away. He had difficulty, though, in getting that rabbit up those steps. I could hear him snarling and complaining. The first I saw was not the rabbit and the head of the cat but the cat's backside and tail as he stepped upwards and backwards on to the window ledge. He then hauled up the corpse with an almighty heave that surprised me, stood with it for a few seconds on the ledge and then, still holding it by a bloody ear, swung it round and almost threw it on to the kitchen floor, leaping down after it with a mighty thump.

Uncle Whiskers was in transports of delight. Never before had he killed anything so big and, perhaps more important still, so delicious to eat. After he had rolled about in his usual manner, purring away like old Harry, I put the rabbit on some newspaper and he proceeded to eat the head. Later on we skinned and cooked the rest, so Uncle Whiskers kept himself in food for a day or two. He caught many, many rabbits after that and there were few things he enjoyed hunting more. There were times during the next twelve months or so when, if Uncle Whiskers was having a lean run of sport, I would sally forth in the late afternoon with a shotgun and knock-off a bunny or two so that he could continue to enjoy one of his favourite meals. But it was the hunting which gave Uncle Whiskers delight and he succeeded, more or less, in exterminating the rats around the house and perhaps even making a slight inroad into the rabbit population. He never brought home a diseased rabbit. This can hardly have been pure coincidence, for blind rabbits in the later stages of this stinking malady would have been easy prey.

As the days drew in and the late autumn nights grew longer we were faced with the dilemma as to whether we should give him complete freedom at night or try to keep him in after dark. He had often been out after sunset but was usually home by midnight or soon after. Now he took to going out around teatime and coming back for supper and a sleep by the fireside, perhaps waking up just as we were preparing to retire and demanding to be let out. There were undoubtedly some dangers in letting him out at night. Apart from the odd cur-dogs, we knew that there were foxes in the woods. Crippled as he was, Uncle Whiskers was unable to avail himself of a cat's methods of escape in an emergency – shinning up the nearest tree – and he surely had no adequate armament to repel an attack from a hungry fox.

There were good grounds for restricting his nocturnal forays. On the other hand, Uncle Whiskers had developed into the best hunting cat we had ever owned and, after one or two initial failures, had become a dab-hand at nailing bunnies. Common prudence is one thing: a safety-first and safety-last policy in life is quite another. So we decided to let him out at any time he wished to go, at least up until the time we went to bed, leaving the kitchen window open so that he could return when he wanted to.

That winter of 1961–2 was a mild and open one, with scarcely any snow worth the mention. On wet or windy nights Uncle Whiskers preferred the warmth of the hearth but on fine nights, particularly if there was a good moon, it was a different story. He would be hunting at dusk and then, after a good sleep, he would be off again about nine or ten o'clock. If, by chance, he caught a rabbit fairly quickly he would come back with it, after which he showed no desire to go out again. But usually it took him at least an hour or two of patient stalking to nail a bunny and, more often than not, he did not succeed at all. So he might be out all night, not putting in an appearance until around breakfast time, when he would be dead-beat and, after eating a good meal, only too ready to curl up and sleep by the fire throughout most of the day.

Although I am sure that it was the right policy to give the cat his freedom, I must admit that there were times when I felt some unease. On more than one winter's morning, if the cat had not returned by two or three o'clock and I happened to wake up, I used to put on a dressing-gown over my pyjamas and sally forth in carpet-slippers to hunt him up. Many was the time, in the quiet small hours, that I padded up and down the frosty lawns, calling Uncle Whiskers by name, poking through this rough patch or that and peering round tree trunks. On moonlight nights, with the grass silvered in heavy rime, the world, even in that unremarkable neighbourhood, could seem very beautiful and remote, with brown owls hooting their lovely music in between their own spells of hunting for the pot. But it could be icily cold and if I failed to find the cat I usually beat a retreat after ten or fifteen minutes. Sometimes I would discover him, however, sitting on the frosted grass, still as a statue, waiting for a rabbit to wander within his limited range. He would never make any move to come to my calling if he was in a hunting mood but he never objected to my picking him up if I did stumble across him, purring with pleasure as I took him back to the house lodged comfortably on my shoulder.

All this good fun and good hunting lasted for Uncle Whiskers for over a year. Then, in the autumn of 1962,

I managed to acquire the lease of a house in a small village not very far distant. But we were not able to move into this new domain until the New Year, so that Uncle Whiskers enjoyed a part of his second winter nailing the rabbits until, at Christmas, the snow came in a big way and put a full stop to his enterprises.

VI

It was a great advantage, both for him and for us, that Uncle Whiskers was an extraordinarily philosophical character. Moreover (and perhaps rather unusually for his tribe) he had no streak of malice in him . . . at least in so far as humans were concerned. If he wanted to go out but, perhaps because we were going shopping we felt it necessary to keep him indoors until our return, it was only necessary, as the cat biffed away at the inside of the door to get out, to say, very firmly, 'No'. He might turn round and gaze at you for a moment, as if he didn't really believe that you meant what you said but, unless he wanted to go out for more urgent reasons than mere pleasure, you only had to repeat the negative and he would plod back to a chair or the fireside. If he had really serious reasons for getting out, he would not go away from the door but would utter a miaow or two, which was meant to convey that he could not be denied. To give him credit, if he was then let out he did get on with any urgent business, although it was necessary to keep an eye on him, for otherwise he would certainly seize the opportunity to beetle off. But if he did go off and you were watching him it was only necessary to shout 'No!' and he would stop in his tracks, stand up on his haunches and look round at you. His glance, under these circumstances, was a somewhat baleful one – a sort of whyd'you-want-to-spoil-my-sport look – but he raised no objections when picked up and brought back indoors.

When we moved to our new home in the middle of January 1963, the snow lay thick. Uncle Whiskers was prepared to put up with almost any sort of weather except thunderstorms and snow. When he was rowing himself along he could scarcely raise his chest off the ground, so that anything more than the thinnest layer of snow was a severe handicap. At that time it lay a foot deep and four times that depth in the drifts and Uncle Whiskers did not like it at all. However, we had a big house and he had a high old time exploring the various new rooms and, best of all, an extensive attic. It was not until a rapid thaw in early March melted the snow that he was at last able really to explore his new terrain. It consisted of over an acre of flower-borders and lawns, with some fine, old yew hedges and a rough paddock of some three acres.

There were few rats, unfortunately, and even rabbits were at a premium but as the spring gave way to summer he had a lot of fun catching shrews and field-mice. There was also a row of stables which not only gave him shelter in wet and windy weather but produced the odd rat that he did manage to nail. In this new home we were unable to leave a window open so that he could come and go as he wished (which had sometimes, in the past, meant as late as breakfast-time on the following morning if sport had been especially good) but the temptations to remain out late were fewer than they had been and, because his territory had been much reduced, I got to know most of his rather numerous hiding-places. Thus, with the aid of a good torch, I would go off hunting him around nightfall or ten o'clock, whichever was the earliest, and could usually find him within ten or fifteen minutes. Sometimes, however, he would elude me by shifting to a completely new hidy-hole and then I made a point of sitting up until he came back. Occasionally this was after midnight and I was not always best pleased, yet it was difficult to feel vexed by a creature that burst into a chorus of purring as soon as one spoke to him.

Despite his missing striking paws and, therefore his apparent lack of the normal feline armament, Uncle Whiskers had the heart of a lion. He could hiss and spit with an intensity that belied his otherwise gentle nature. I never saw any dog get the better of him: although he never succeeded in chasing any stray curs off the premises, he never gave an inch to them, whether they barked or snarled or no. He used to sit up on his hind legs and spit like a barmaid. As to cats, he couldn't abide any of them, at least until he was taken into a household where one was already established. Perhaps not unnaturally, intruding cats always seemed to be nonplussed when he reared on his hindquarters, looking rather like a penguin, and at the same time making it clear in the most unfriendly language that they were not welcome. If the intruding cat still stood its ground he would quickly crouch and then spring at it, descending upon it from above. Most cats fled but if it did come to a bit of really good in-fighting, Uncle Whiskers fell back on his two great assets: powerful jaws and a fine set of sharp teeth. Throughout his long life he retained perfect teeth and even in his old age they never became brown and stained, which is unusual in a cat.

During the three years in this new home he kept all other cats off our three or four acres. There was a small, under-nourished black female that used to creep round to the back-door whenever his lordship was not in sight, for we took pity on this grossly neglected creature by giving her at least one square meal a day, with a saucerful of milk to wash it down. As far as possible we tried to ensure that this poor waif did not meet Uncle Whiskers, although he was well aware of her visits because, long after she had gone, he would sniff around the kitchen with every evidence of disgust.

Sometimes, in spite of our efforts, the two did encounter one another. Uncle Whiskers went to the utmost pains to ensure that the meetings were as brief as possible. He would spit and, as the black lady fled, he was after her in a series of leaps and bounds that would have done credit to a kangaroo. Nor was she really able to outpace him with her four good legs until she had disappeared through a thick yew hedge on the boundary of our garden and so into her own backyard.

At this time Uncle Whiskers was just about in his prime. He had developed the most enormous hams and his prodigious leaps when in full pursuit of this enemy were quite astonishing, especially if he was on a level surface, such as one of the lawns. Over short distances, fired with the enthusiasm of pursuing a quarry 'in view', he could clear eight feet at one bound and, somehow or other, he contrived to land not on his chest but on his hind feet, so that he sprang up almost instantly into his next leap. Over a distance of ten or twelve yards he could go like a bomb. It was a magnificent sight to watch, utterly different to his normally rather slow gait as he rowed himself along on his wonky foreleg.

I only knew of two occasions in his long life when Uncle Whiskers was worsted. One was when he was chasing the black female back to her own dunghill. He was so incensed on this occasion that, instead of calling off his pursuit on reaching the boundary of the yew hedge, he carried it on into the garden of his vexatious enemy's owners. It was summer and it just so happened that the black cat's neglectful owners were in the garden at the time. They raised cries of anguish which could only have been justified had they been devoted to their cat or if Uncle Whiskers was killing her, as I have little doubt he would have liked to have done to get rid of her bothersome trespasses on his own preserves. In the face of the combined shrieks of a whole family, Uncle Whiskers lost his nerve, turned, and made a run for the safety of the yew hedge. His smart emergence on his own side was followed, literally, by half a brick hurled in his direction. Considering his crippled state this struck me as a particularly wicked act, for had the jagged and heavy missile hit Uncle Whiskers it might have done him mortal harm. Anyway, he had enough sense to learn from this nasty experience, for on subsequent occasions when he chased off the black cat he always called off his pursuit in the safe, thick cover of the yew hedge.

The only other occasion when Uncle Whiskers beat a retreat had occurred back at the big house. I was watching him early one September morning, plodding back past the swimming-pool and over the lawns when he was dive-bombed by a pair of screaming swallows. As they dashed down on him they came very low. He stood up on his haunches, making futile swipes with his flipper and then, unable to stand their screaming attentions any longer, he bounded away to the terrace and the safety of the house at his very best speed.

Uncle Whiskers was a good 'trencherman' but, unlike the majority of his kind, he was not greedy. I suspect that his tastebuds were as good as his outstanding 'nose' and certainly throughout the last half of his life he was a first-class feline gourmet. If he found there was no alternative (which was not often) he would eat some of the proprietary brands of cat food but he thrived on variety. His mainstays consisted of liver, either scalded or raw, raw shin of beef, kidneys and hearts, but he would enjoy almost any kind of meat. He was especially partial to game of any kind. The prospect of pheasant or grouse as he 'nosed' them in the cooking would set him off into purring ecstasies of anticipation and hare, hot or cold, he rated very highly.

He was choosey in the matter of fish, not putting any value on cod or coley but very partial to herring or haddock. He liked cured and smoked foods, such as Arbroath smokies, kippers and smoked salmon, not to mention fresh salmon and sea-trout. Some shellfish – freshly shelled shrimps and prawns, for examples – he adored and freshly dressed crabmeat he regarded as one of the greatest delicacies of all. Although he loved to anticipate, by smell, the pleasures of a good meal in the offing, he never pestered to be fed and he never rushed his meals, as most cats and dogs do. When you put his plate down he would waddle over to it, purring happily, take several long, appraising sniffs and then settle himself down comfortably before starting to eat.

I cannot now remember when Uncle Whiskers first took to strong drink but over the last half of his life he became quite a wine-bibber. The 'plop' of a drawn cork would always stimulate his interest, even to the extent of rousing him from a deep slumber. The drier the wine the better he was pleased. He was usually rationed to eight drops, presented to him on each finger-tip in turn, after which his satisfaction was shown by much licking of chops. Perhaps best of all he relished a very dry sherry or a good port. He thought nothing of either beer or cider but rated straight malt whisky and brandy pretty highly. I should make it clear that Uncle Whiskers was strictly rationed in the amount of booze that he was allowed.

In the summer of 1964, when Uncle Whiskers was five years old, I took up an editorial position on a lively, weekly sporting publication, *Shooting Times & Country Magazine*, which at that time had its offices in London. I now had to face a long train journey five days a week and was glad that, by nature, I had always been an early riser. I used to leave home at 6.30 a.m. to cycle the two miles to my local station and, with luck, I arrived home about 7.30 in the evening.

Except at week-ends, therefore, I did not see so much of Uncle Whiskers. An added difficulty arose because my wife was already suffering from the onset of arthritis in both hips, so I used to get my own breakfast before setting off. Uncle Whiskers always got up when I did, usually accompanying me to the bathroom each morning, perhaps buoyed up by the prospect of getting his breakfast earlier than usual. Whilst the bath-water was running and I was shaving, the cat would patrol the large bathroom and then sit up on his haunches to take a 'dekko' out of the window, perhaps to weigh up the weather prospects for the coming day. But as soon as I got into the bath he would stump his way over, taking up position on the bath-mat. From time to time he would rise up on his haunches, peering wide-eyed over the edge of the bath to see what all the splashing was about. He gave me the impression, as he stared down on me plunged in the water, that he considered the whole exercise as nothing more than just another charming piece of human nonsense. Perhaps if Uncle Whiskers had been able to voice his thoughts he might have agreed that it was reasonable to get soaking wet when hunting in heavy rain but throwing yourself into water was madness. Cleanliness, he would probably have agreed, was certainly necessary but what was wrong with spit and lick?

During the next twelve months, except at week-ends, I saw relatively little of Uncle Whiskers. However, as he grew older he grew more endearing in his ways. If he was indoors when I arrived home in the evening, then no matter where he was he would come stumping along to greet me as soon as he heard my voice. The greeting, apart from his putting in an appearance, consisted of very loud purring, easily audible when he was still a long way off, and tail held proudly erect, waving from side to side, as he approached. Arriving at my feet he would immediately sit up on his haunches and rub his face against my trouser-leg. He always reckoned, I think, to be tossed on to my shoulder and get his tummy tickled. I don't think he was ever disappointed.

The older he grew, the stronger became his habit of greeting everybody who came into the house. He recognized 'regulars' by their voices. Whenever we had guests staying overnight he was well aware that they had not departed. First thing in the morning, often before we wanted to be on the move ourselves, he would get down from the bed and bang on the door to be let out. Once the door was opened he would stump along to the guests' room, sit up outside and bang the door so sharply with his flipper that those inside often mistook it for a human knock and answered, 'Come in'. As Uncle Whiskers couldn't oblige by coming in, he would go on rapping until a puzzled guest (if he were a stranger) got out of bed and opened the door to see who was outside. As soon as the door opened Uncle Whiskers stumped in and, putting on a rare turn of speed, reached the end of the bed and jumped up on it almost before the guest had realized what was happening. He would then sit bolt upright and purr away fit to bust. There were few visitors who failed to succumb to the VIP treatment.

With two necessary operations in the offing, my wife returned to Hampshire, where she would be among her relatives and old friends. I remained based at our old home for the time being, for several reasons. The lease I had entered into had several years to run, for one thing. Then again, although my office was in London there were rumours in the air that it might be moved into Berkshire and I was naturally anxious to know the outcome before making any firm plans for the future. There was also the problem of Uncle Whiskers, now six years old and in the prime of his life.

I have mentioned the row of stables adjoining the house.

Because I had to be away all day, except at week-ends, I converted one of the stables by substituting a wire-mesh frame, on hinges and with a latch, for the bottom section of the half-deck door. Although I had to be away at half-past six in the morning, Uncle Whiskers, bursting with energy after a night's sleep, was always happy to be on the move early, so now I used to let him out at five o'clock, before bathing and shaving. When I got my own breakfast I also prepared Uncle Whiskers'. He was seldom far enough away not to be able to hear the clatter of crockery and was usually back on the doorstep by the time I had his meal prepared. I usually took his meal into the dining-room so that we could breakfast together.

At this age Uncle Whiskers seemed to have developed an almost touching faith that, whatever happened, everything would turn out all right in the long run. Before I set off for London at half-past six I prepared him another meal and took this, together with a saucerful of milk, to the prepared stable. Then I had to collect the cat, put him in the stable and secure the door. The cat had plenty of room here, as well as straw on which to snug himself down. The, sun shone in through the wire-mesh frame in the mornings so that in fine weather he could sunbathe for a few hours each day. With luck I used to arrive back on my cycle some thirteen hours later. It was still summer, so that there was plenty of daylight left. I called to Uncle Whiskers as I rode round to the back of the house and the first thing I did after propping up my cycle was to hurry down the garden to release the cat from his imprisonment. He would be standing up high on his hind legs, his maimed forepaw propped against the wire-mesh, purring with pleasure. I used to greet him with two or three minutes of pure fussing as he lay along my crooked arm, his purring song rattling louder and louder as he biffed his face into my left ear. No cat I have ever known purred louder or for

86

longer periods. He could purr at full-blast for as much as an hour and almost anything was likely to provoke him into song.

When I put him down I went back to the house to prepare our evening meals. Uncle Whiskers appeared to appreciate that this usually took anything from twenty minutes to half an hour, so he roamed around for a period before landing, punctually, on the kitchen doorstep, often still purring!

After he had finished his supper he would sally forth for an evening's hunting. There were few rabbits about but he still succeeded in nailing the odd one, stumbling and lurching back with it, depositing the corpse on the tiled kitchen floor before coming up the passage to attract my attention to come along and inspect his latest trophy. I used to leave Uncle Whiskers out as late as was practicable, bearing in mind the early start next day. It was usually dark when I went hunting for him, looking in one hidy-hole after another with a torch until I located him. Normally I picked him up within four or five minutes but sometimes, when he had discovered some new spot, it might take half an hour. He seldom gave himself away deliberately but he never demurred when I did find him and always started singing as I carried him back to the house. At week-ends, of course, he was able to spend all his time in the garden except in foul weather.

The situation grew more difficult as the long summer came to an end and autumn ushered in the shorter days. Soon it was almost twilight by the time I returned from London in the evenings. This, however, did not upset Uncle Whiskers because he enjoyed hunting in the dark perhaps even more than he did in daylight. Cold and frosty weather never seemed to upset him. Nevertheless, I was glad when an acquaintance of mine came to stay with me in the house. He was in need of temporary accommodation and it certainly suited me to provide it. He was a booking-clerk at my local station and he worked different shifts on alternate weeks. On one shift he went off even before I did but was home early in the afternoon; on the other he would be at home all morning and returned from his work around bedtime. With the onset of winter it was really too cold to put Uncle Whiskers in the stable but my new arrangement meant that he could either have the morning or else most of an afternoon roaming around, as well as the late evening after I had got back. For the rest of the time he was in the house, contented enough to sleep the hours away.

My offices were moved from London to Maidenhead. I was now only home at week-ends but my acquaintance looked after Uncle Whiskers during the week. None the less I was beginning to steel myself to the unattractive prospect of having to part company with Uncle Whiskers. To cut a long story short, within the next few months I succeeded in buying my way out of my lease of a house that had become a millstone round my neck. Better still, I was fortunate to have an old friend, then living in a village not far away, who was willing to take over Uncle Whiskers. She had known the cat ever since we had first had him and I knew that she could give him a better home than I could hope to do in difficult circumstances. During the week I was going to have to live in a town working-flat. I do not think that it is reasonable to keep an active cat in any flat, let alone in a built-up area and it would surely have been an intolerable ordeal for an adventurous cat like Uncle Whiskers.

Uncle Whiskers, philosophical as ever, took to the change just as a duck takes to water. My friend had a cat of her own, by the name of Sammy. Not unnaturally this Sammy resented the arrival of a strange cat, more especially one that sat up erect on his haunches and spat at him. Within a day, however, they both settled down to a harmonious relationship which lasted to the end. Uncle Whiskers, however – as was fitting for a senior partner – was the boss of the outfit.

VII

It was inevitable that I now saw Uncle Whiskers only occasionally but he was obviously having a great life. His new owner had built him a pen in the garden (roofed-in!) in which he was put whenever she went out, lest he should stray on to the road that ran past the house and land himself in trouble. At all other times he had full use of a fairly large and pleasant garden. There was an absence of both rats and rabbits but the cat was now in his eighth year and seemed to be content with chasing smaller fry, such as shrews. As he grew older he spent more and more time sleeping, outdoors in the summers and indoors in the winters.

He developed into a real character in his new village. Passing strangers would gaze over the wall, astonished to see a cat sitting up on his haunches for minutes on end, gazing round at the wonderful world about him and with only one gammy foreleg dangling across his chest. Everybody got to know Uncle Whiskers and on occasions, not all that infrequent, when he contrived to escape into the big wide world I was told that anything up to a dozen folk would join in the hunt to retrieve him.

The cottage which was now his home was separated from a small church and a larger churchyard only by a narrow lane. On one occasion when he had escaped unnoticed and the search party had apparently looked everywhere without success, his new owner, ferreting about in the unkempt churchyard, suddenly saw an orange face shoot up above the rim of a big tombstone. It is probably being very anthropomorphic, but I know from long experience that on occasions such as these Uncle Whiskers appeared to adopt a very curious attitude which seemed to convey the message that he really just could not understand what all the fuss and bother was about.

When his new owner finally retired from work she moved up to Cumberland to a house that was far removed from any roads, surrounded by a pretty garden and acres upon acres of green hill-pastures intersected by stone walls. Uncle Whiskers, now more than ten years old, suddenly came into his own again, for he could once more roam about almost at will and his last years were very happy ones, even if he was now getting a bit old and stiff in the limbs. He was in his twelfth year when he caught and killed his last rabbit. I wish I had been there, for I was told that he made his usual song and dance after the kill. But, rabbits apart, there were plenty of field voles and shrews to test his hunting skills in the autumn of his days.

He was over twelve when, whilst he was sitting sunning himself in an open window overlooking the lawn, a rabbit had the temerity to parade in front of him. He had the advantage of starting from a ledge two or three feet higher than the rabbit. The temptation was irresistible to one of the greatest of feline hunters, even if he was now somewhat long in the tooth. Girding his hind limbs he released himself into one almighty spring, clearing a measured nine feet from take-off to touch-down. But the rabbit was too quick for him and all he got for his pains was a mouthful of fur; had he possessed two good striking paws the rabbit would not have stood an earthly chance.

I only saw Uncle Whiskers when rare opportunity offered. Sometimes months passed before we were able once again to exchange greetings. However, he never forgot my voice and, unlike the days when we had been together, he would now come loping out of a hidy-hole as soon as I called to him, rowing himself along to greet me with obvious eagerness and, as usual, purring away like a rattling nightjar.

There was one glorious if short-lived Indian Summer for both of us. In the October before the cat's death, his new owner wrote to me to say that she was going away for a week. Would I like to enjoy the use of her house and, at the same time, look after Uncle Whiskers and her other cat? I leapt at the chance. The weather was perfect throughout. Few things are better than glorious sunshine in lovely countryside. After a break of over five years, it was fun to have Uncle Whiskers to myself again. The Old Man was in great form, too, prowling around in the sunshine from dawn to dusk, priming his still healthy appetite.

I suppose it could be said that it was the cruel accident which half-crippled him that was the making of Uncle Whiskers. Beyond any doubt he possessed intelligence far above that of the normal cat, yet it was the crippling effects of his accident that had thrown him on to his own resources, making it necessary for him to think out solutions to all sorts of problems with which any ordinary cat is never faced. I believe that this story of his life shows that, although the way was often hard for him, he usually triumphed in the end.

For a time the effects of his accident made him far more dependent upon human aid than is the case with most cats. It was natural, perhaps, that he developed an affection for those with whom he associated every day and who provided for his needs. However, he was seldom nervous in the company of others unless they were deliberately aggressive. Anybody who was foolish enough to try to take gross liberties with him was likely to finish up with four bleeding punctures in one of his or her fingers. In his later years he fairly revelled in company. Whenever strangers arrived in the house he woke up and took a keen interest in them, no doubt hoping to get a fair share of the lime-light. Even those who normally disliked cats fell for Uncle Whiskers. If he got a lot of pleasure out of his life, in the living of it he also gave much pleasure to others. Those who got to know him will not easily forget him nor will they ever see the like of him again. Uncle Whiskers was unique.

Envoi

Uncle Whiskers died on 4 October 1972. He was in his fourteenth year and had enjoyed twelve years of life, mostly very active, since the accident that nearly killed him in September 1960. He had been fit and well throughout his last spring and summer and had enjoyed a warm and sunny August sitting out in the sun or seeking some hidy-hole in the shade to sleep away the hot hours of the afternoons. It was not until late in that month that he went off his food and developed an unwonted lethargy that began to cause concern.

I saw him early in September and agreed that it was time to seek the advice of the vet. Although he had twenty miles to come the vet arrived within the hour. Was this the end, I wondered. Uncle Whiskers, who had developed extraordinary confidence in everybody in his old age, started to purr happily as the vet handled him but winced a bit when prodded round the kidneys. These organs were enlarged and the vet pronounced that the cat was suffering from anaemia. But the vet was satisfied that he was in no immediate pain or discomfort. It was, in his professional view, worth trying an injection, which by violently stimulating the liver, might afford him a new lease of life.

It was a coolish day for the time of year and a fire was lit for the benefit of the invalid. Uncle Whiskers always adored open fires, with the logs crackling and the flames roaring up the chimney. This time however, it was altogether different. He was seized with successive spasms of vomiting; long after he had nothing more to bring up he went on retching with a violence that was painful to watch. He sat crouched uncomfortably, staring in front of him with wild, dilated pupils although every time he was spoken to by name he would twitch the tip of his tail in acknowledgement.

In the afternoon, when the retching abated, the poor creature was seized with equally violent fits of colic. Ill as he was, he would lurch across the room to evacuate his bowels in a box in the passage. I noticed for the first time that his only two sound legs seemed now to be partially paralysed. I forsook my room at the village inn in order to spend the night with the cat. There was little that I could do to make him comfortable, except to keep the fire going. The bouts of colic eased off as the night wore on but Uncle Whiskers was very thirsty and never slept at all. He sat open-eyed, gazing into space, almost as if in a coma. It crossed my mind many times during that long night's vigil that in the morning the vet must be summoned to put him out of his misery. He never once cried out but his behaviour was so strange and he was now so obviously physically exhausted that death would surely be a merciful release.

As a grey dawn broke, however, Uncle Whiskers came to life again. He ate a little Brand's essence of beef, washed himself rather vaguely and started purring. The pupils of his eyes were less dilated and later in the morning, for the first time in over twenty-four hours, he went to sleep curled up on his side. By the afternoon he seemed refreshed, would break out into a roaring purr of delight when spoken to or stroked and, finally, insisted upon going exploring in the garden. The paralysis of his hind limbs had disappeared completely. Uncle Whiskers was himself again.

The next day he really was himself. He ate like a trooper: three good platefuls of fresh lamb's liver and, between spells of sleeping, much outdoor activity sparked off by a shrew which he narrowly failed to pounce upon as it popped into the safety of a stone drain. During the next day or two he faced life with renewed vigour, as if he had never ailed at all, rolling about in the sunshine in that ecstatic mood of glorious self-confidence that recalled the days when he had been a mighty slayer of rats.

The Indian Summer was short-lived. I happened to be in the neighbourhood in the last week of September and took the chance to see him again. He rose up in purring greeting but he was again off his food. The vet returned and another injection was given. This time there was no sickness but it made no difference to his listlessness. If you tickled his tummy he would still stretch out in delight and purr away. He looked in fair fettle, his fur as soft and sleek as ever but he was growing old and weary.

I never saw Uncle Whiskers again. On the evening of 3 October he was clearly very ill. All night long, I heard, he could not settle. Early the next morning he was obviously in pain and the vet was summoned by telephone. Yet the old spirit still fired the dying hunter. He insisted on being let out into the autumn sunshine, lurching over the grass on half-paralysed limbs, to reach one of his favourite sunny corners below an ash tree. There he lay, occasionally crying softly in pain, comforted by his devoted guardian, baffled and bewildered by this final struggle against hopeless odds which he could not even begin to understand.

The vet came very soon. The merciful injection was given and in a matter of seconds, held in the arms of one of his best and most faithful friends, all the pain and travail came to an end. Uncle Whiskers lies now, peacefully enough, high up in the Cumberland fells, close under the shelter of a stone wall that will shield him from the worst of the westerly gales. On clear nights in winter the stars of Orion, the great heavenly hunter, will ride across the sky, brown owls will hoot in the ash tree above his grave and rabbits may scamper and play on the silvery, frosted grass. Uncle Whiskers, in his last eternal sleep, will mind them no more.